An ode to a mucky home

I like writing poems and songs in my spare time. I get an idea and let it splash around in my brain, and suddenly, I'm singing. This time, my song is about my ideal home.

> How I love a mucky home,
> Mucky home,
> Mucky home!
> How I love a mucky home,
> One with a water view.
>
> I love a house that drips a bit,
> Drips a bit,
> Drips a bit!
> I love a house that drips a bit,
> With gunk and grime and goo.
>
> I love a home with bugs nearby,
> Bugs nearby,
> Bugs nearby!
> I love a home with bugs nearby
> If I can grab a few!

Look for all of the adventures in Room 26

Exploring
according to
Og the Frog

Betty G. Birney

PUFFIN BOOKS

To the dedicated humans

working around the globe to protect amphibian populations,

which are declining at an alarming rate

PUFFIN BOOKS
An imprint of Penguin Random House LLC, New York

First published in the United States of America by G. P. Putnam's Sons, 2019
Published by Puffin Books, an imprint of Penguin Random House LLC, 2020

Visit us online at penguinrandomhouse.com

THE LIBRARY OF CONGRESS HAS CATALOGED THE G. P. PUTNAM'S SONS EDITION AS FOLLOWS:
Names: Birney, Betty G., author.
Title: Exploring according to Og the Frog / Betty G. Birney.
Description: New York, NY: G. P. Putnam's Sons, [2019] |
Summary: Og the Frog finally gets the chance to explore human world and to assist
Humphrey the Hamster in helping their human friends in Room 26.
Identifiers: LCCN 2018028700 (print) | LCCN 2018035099 (ebook) |
ISBN 9781524739980 (ebook) | ISBN 9781524739973 (hardcover)
Subjects: | CYAC: Adventure and adventurers—Fiction. | Frogs—Fiction. | Schools—Fiction.
Classification: LCC PZ7.B5229 (ebook) | LCC PZ7.B5229 Exp 2019 (print) | DDC [Fic]—dc23
LC record available at https://lccn.loc.gov/2018028700

Puffin Books ISBN 9781524739997

Printed in the United States of America

Design by Eileen Savage
Text set in Warnock Pro

1 3 5 7 9 10 8 6 4 2

CONTENTS
. . . .

1

Boxed In

· · · · · · · · · · · · · · · · ·

There's so much to see in the swamp: blue sky, mucky brown water, green lily pads, and all kinds of colorful (and yummy) insects. As our teacher, Granny Greenleaf, told us little tads in the swamp, "If you want a view, the swamp is for you!" Why would anyone ever want to leave? And even if someone did, how would he begin? As a young tad, I had no idea.

In Room 26, the view is very different from the swamp!

I have only lived at Longfellow School for a short time, but luckily, I'm a clever frog, and I caught on to life in the classroom in a hurry. Right now, though, I am looking at something strange even for a classroom—a sea of boxes.

Boxes are everywhere!

One thing I've learned is that although frogs and other swamp creatures like me love living out in the open near water, humans prefer to live in boxes. Their houses may all look different, but to my froggy eyes, they are all boxes, divided into smaller boxes called rooms.

Not only do humans live in boxes, so do hamsters!

At least Humphrey does, and he's the only hamster I know. He lives in a box with sides made of bars, called a cage. It sits on a table by the window, right next to my tank.

I, at least, have glass walls and some water, but it's still a lot different from the way I lived back in the swamp not so long ago.

And now our teacher, Mrs. Brisbane, has the class building a little town with houses and buildings made from—you guessed it—boxes.

As we say in the swamp, "Whatever makes you hoppy!"

"SQUEAK-SQUEAK-SQUEAK!" my neighbor shouts.

Humphrey's squeaks sound cheerful, maybe because they've named the little town Humphreyville. I'm never sure what he's thinking, though, because I haven't understood a word he's said so far! And he clearly doesn't understand my green frog "BOINGs."

The humans don't, either. They don't understand that "BOING-BOING" might mean "thank you." Or "BOING-*BOING*" might mean "good job!" They think one boing is like another, which isn't true.

At least I've been able to figure out what humans are saying.

"Don't forget the small details of your house," Mrs. Brisbane reminds the big tads. "And think about the other town buildings as well, like the school and city hall."

More boxes.

Mandy Payne works on the biggest box of all. "I'm making a huge, fancy house with lots of windows," she says. "And my own room."

"What kind of dinosaur can jump higher than a house?" Kirk asks.

"You tell us," Mrs. Brisbane says. She knows Kirk likes to tell jokes.

"All of them!" he answers. "Houses can't jump."

BING-BANG-BOING! How does he think of these things?

The class settles down, and I look around the room. As usual, everything is bright and clean. (Especially after a man named Aldo comes in with his broom and mop each weeknight.)

It's nothing like the swamp, which is a wonderland of mud, pond scum and damp grass.

I don't think most humans would like to live in the swamp, but many other creatures do. Not just frogs, but slithery snakes, lizards and turtles, cranes and eagles, bats, owls, and tasty treats like dragonflies, mosquitoes and—yum—crickets.

We frogs like a home that's a bit damp and mucky. I

don't even mind some glorious goo. As our teacher, Granny Greenleaf, taught us, "A place that's wetter is a place that's better. Get too dry, and it's *bye-bye*!"

I think about the mud, and after a while, I hear a melody in my head. Before I even know it, I've thought up a song.

I like writing poems and songs in my spare time. I get an idea and let it splash around in my brain, and suddenly, I'm singing. This time, my song is about my ideal home.

How I love a mucky home,
Mucky home,
Mucky home!
How I love a mucky home,
One with a water view.

I love a house that drips a bit,
Drips a bit,
Drips a bit!
I love a house that drips a bit,
With gunk and grime and goo.

I love a home with bugs nearby,
Bugs nearby,
Bugs nearby!
I love a home with bugs nearby
If I can grab a few!

Don't get the wrong idea. My tank isn't bad. It's half land and half water, so I can take a dip anytime I feel a little dry. Mrs. Brisbane's husband, Bert, has added a lot of greenery, and I get good treats (though not as many juicy, wiggly crickets as I'd like).

The bell rings for recess, and it's time for me to relax in the water and let my mind roam free.

Float. Doze. *Be.*

Today, my mind roams back to McKenzie's Marsh, where I used to live before I was frognapped and brought here to Longfellow School. My name was Bongo then, but the students in Miss Loomis's class didn't know that, so they called me Og. I don't mind.

I was scared when the man took me from the swamp, but I don't think he knew he was doing a bad thing. In fact, he looked at me and said, "You are a good-looking frog. A real prince of a frog!" A prince—really? Did he know something I don't know?

Then he gave me to his grandson, who brought me to school to be a classroom pet.

Life wasn't all lily pads and lah-de-dah there in the swamp. I was always trying to catch enough food to fill my belly . . . without ending up as dinner for a bigger creature! Here in Room 26, I have no enemies, at least so far. I don't have to hunt because humans throw food into my tank.

But sometimes I get a tiny bit *bored*. I keep busy

swimming, hopping and watching my furry neighbor. Of course, I also write songs and poems.

My memories of the swamp fade away when the students—I think of them as big tadpoles—return from recess. Mrs. Brisbane tells them to get out their math books, and the door opens.

"Welcome, Paul," Mrs. Brisbane says. "Please come right in."

Hey, I know that boy! It's Paul Fletcher.

"Class, some of you may know Paul Fletcher from Miss Loomis's class. He is going to be coming into our class for math," our teacher says.

"Hi, friend!" I boing. He is usually in Room 27, where I lived for a little while. I liked it there, but a bullfrog named George was there first, and he badmouthed me from morning until night.

"RUM-RUM. RUM-RUM!" he'd repeat over and over.

He was as bad as Louie the Loudmouth, the leader of the bullying bullfrogs back in the swamp. Miss Loomis had to shout her lessons to be heard over George.

Paul passes by my tank on his way to his chair.

"Hi, Og," he says softly. "Glad to see you."

"BOING!" I answer softly. "Same here."

Some of the big tads make whispery noises, and Heidi points out that Paul is a year younger than the students in our class. That makes Paul stare down at the floor.

Mrs. Brisbane explains that even though he's a little bit younger, he is an excellent math student, so he will be studying with them.

And she's right. Even with George rum-rumming in Room 27, I could see Paul was good with numbers.

I don't know a lot about classroom math. In the swamp, all I needed to know about numbers is that one bullfrog is one bullfrog too many, and the best way to measure things is a hop, skip and a jump! But humans like to solve more difficult problems.

Mrs. Brisbane gives her students a tricky one that day. I even hear Art moan. The big tads work hard, but I can see that he and Mandy and a few other big tads are having trouble solving it by the way they chew their pencils and frown.

Paul has an easier time and finishes quickly.

"Way to go!" I shout, making a big splash when he puts his pencil down.

When math is over and Paul leaves, Heidi whispers to Gail, "What is he, some kind of brainiac?"

"More like a know-it-all," Gail mutters.

Kirk nods. "A real show-off."

A know-it-all and a show-off? I'd say Paul is on the ball and a smart student.

Mrs. Brisbane overhears them and shakes her head. "There'll be none of that talk here," she says firmly. "Everyone in this classroom is good at something. For Paul, it's math. So no more name calling. *Ever.*"

The room gets quiet and stays that way.

The next day, Paul returns for math.

Mrs. Brisbane is writing on the board, and she doesn't hear Mandy whisper, "Here comes Mr. Know-It-All."

"Watch it!" I warn her. "BOING-BOING!"

Paul keeps his head down, listens to the teacher and solves the problems.

I remember something Granny Greenleaf once said back in the swamp. "Hold your head high, even when you're feeling low."

I've tried it, and it works. Sometimes, when you're feeling low down, it's hard to keep your chin up, but it makes you feel better. Stronger. Hoppier.

"Hold your head high!" I tell Paul.

Unfortunately, the big tads laugh. They're laughing at my boings, but I can see that Paul thinks they're laughing at him. Now I've made things worse when I was trying to make them better!

I feel as useless as a dragonfly with waterlogged wings.

Then Humphrey speaks up, too. "SQUEAK-SQUEAK-SQUEAK-SQUEAK-*SQUEAK*!"

The tads laugh again, and Paul's face gets redder.

"Class, stop laughing right now! We're here to learn,

and you're upsetting Humphrey and Og," Mrs. Brisbane says.

For once I understand what Humphrey is thinking. He doesn't like the big tads' rudeness, and neither do I. BING-BANG-*BOING*! I think we're making progress.

Throughout the week, the big tads are as busy as beavers working on Humphreyville, which grows a little bit every day.

More boxes are added to the town along with a patch of green labeled OG THE FROG NATURE PRESERVE. I'm glad they didn't name a box after me!

When Paul comes in, some of the students roll their eyes. But at least they keep quiet, while Paul keeps his head down (which is the opposite of holding your head high).

Then comes Friday, the day when Mrs. Brisbane announces which student will take Humphrey home for the weekend.

Everybody always wants to take Humphrey home for the weekend.

I stay back in Room 26. Mrs. Brisbane says it's more difficult to take me home because my tank is so heavy. And I don't need to have food and water as often as Humphrey. For a small creature who is mostly fur, he sure eats a lot! And what he doesn't eat, he saves in his cheek pouch.

If you think eating crickets like I do is icky, imagine storing food in your cheeks! Eww!

Mandy is not so pleased when she learns she won't be taking Humphrey home. "I never get to take him," she complains. Mrs. Brisbane points out that she has not returned a signed permission slip from her parents, which makes Mandy as flustered as a snapping turtle with weak jaws.

Seth lets out a whoop when he learns that he will have Humphrey for the weekend. He is a friendly human, but he has a hard time sitting still. He taps and twitches. He jiggles and wiggles. Sometimes I get tired just watching him!

I think Humphrey will have his paws full at Seth's house this weekend, while I will have plenty of time to think.

Maybe I'll figure out what I can do to help Paul feel comfortable in our class.

After Aldo leaves Friday night (thanks to him for giving me some extra food), I have the classroom all to myself, and now I have a clear view of the houses in Humphreyville. They're all different, but every one is made from a box.

My fellow swamp creatures live in many kinds of homes. There are nests for the birds, while bats like a comfy crack in a tree. Beavers think big, building huge lodges out of wood.

Other creatures—like me and my frog friends—find our shelter under logs and leaves wherever we roam. That's right, I am a roaming kind of creature. Or at least I was before I became a classroom pet and got boxed in.

But here in my nice clean tank, at least I have some water, rocks and a bit of muck.

How many times did Granny Greenleaf tell us, "Whatever you do, wherever you are, make the most of your time, and you'll go far!"?

I get busy on my exercise routine so that even if I'm stuck in a tank, I'll still be the great leaper I was back in the swamp. First, I splash. I mean, I really *splash*.

Next come my jumping jacks. With each leap, I try to go a little higher. While I do, I think of my best frog friend in the swamp, Jumpin' Jack. We were both high jumpers, *and* I could understand everything he said, unlike my new friend Humphrey!

Push-ups are next on my list, followed by a series of giant leaps across my rock.

To finish, I swim so many laps, I lose count. Maybe I should pay more attention in math class, the way Paul does.

By the time I finish, it's already starting to get dark outside. After all, it's winter.

I relax on my rock and take some deep breaths. Time to Float. Doze. *Be.*

I am so relaxed after all that exercise that I fall fast asleep.

When I wake up, it's morning. Right away, I realize something is strange. The light is different than on other days. I turn to look toward the window, and I see it: snow.

I sit and stare for a long time because it's so white and so beautiful.

If I were still in the swamp, I'd be taking a long winter's nap. It's called hibernating.

I guess Jumpin' Jack and all my green frog pals in the swamp are hibernating now. They're not watching the fluffy snowflakes silently paint the world white. Think of all they're missing!

As I stare out at the white world, a little song starts forming in my brain.

It's a quiet song, like a lullaby, and I imagine I'm singing it to my friends.

> Rock-a-bye, frog friends,
> Down in the ice,
> I hope the dreams
> You're dreaming are nice.
>
> When you awaken,
> Down in the deep,
> Think about all
> You missed while asleep!

The song seems sad, but surprisingly, I feel a whole lot better! (Singing can do that for you. Try it!)

It wasn't my choice to move from the swamp to the classroom, but I suddenly see it as a great opportunity that few frogs ever have.

Unlike my friends sleeping in the swamp, I'm fully awake to see winter. I have dozens of new friends of strange but interesting species. Not only humans, but a *hamster*! Up until now, I thought Granny Greenleaf and wise old Uncle Chinwag knew everything, but believe me, they've never even heard of a hamster.

I have seen some amazing things back in the swamp. I once saw a water moccasin tie himself in a knot. And I saw a bullfrog with hiccups leap across six lily pads *and* the back of a snapping turtle, and he lived to tell about it.

But now a door has opened to the world of humans (and hamsters), and I, an adventurous, roaming green frog, would like to explore it. I want to go where no green frog has dared to go before.

I'll make a big splash! I may even become a legend like Sir Hiram Hopwell, the most famous frog ever.

Tomorrow, when the big tads and Mrs. Brisbane return to Room 26, I will be all ears (even though you can't see them) and all eyes (which are large and alert) so I can learn more than any frog ever has about all kinds of humans and the human world.

On Monday morning, I feel like a different frog. I'm rested, in great shape and ready to begin my mission.

When Seth brings Humphrey back to our shelf by the window, he says, "Thanks, Humphrey. I had the best weekend *ever!*"

Later I notice something new. Seth starts to fidget, but Humphrey squeaks, and Seth settles down. Then it happens again.

I'm puzzling over that when the door opens and the principal of Longfellow School, Mr. Morales, walks in. Whenever he enters, my classmates snap to attention. Even Humphrey rushes up his tree branch for a better look.

And Mr. Morales always wears the most interesting ties! Once he even wore one with funny frogs on it.

He tells Mrs. Brisbane that he's stopped in to see how Humphreyville is coming along.

"SQUEAK-SQUEAK-SQUEAK!" my neighbor says.

"Seems like a great place to live," Mr. Morales says after looking around. "Good work."

After he leaves, our teacher assigns the big tads jobs in the classroom. I don't understand most of them, like "line monitor" or "pencil patrol." There are no familiar jobs like "cricket catcher" or "helpful hopper." But when Miranda is given the job of "animal keeper," I know that she'll be looking after Humphrey and me.

That's a good thing, because Miranda is as responsible as Cousin Lucy Lou, who never showed up late for Granny

Greenleaf's class and never missed a leaping practice. She wasn't a high hopper, but she tried harder than any of us.

Good old Lucy Lou. I wonder if she misses me.

When the bell rings at the end of the day, Miranda comes over to my tank and bends down so we are eye to eye.

"Og, I'm going to take really good care of you!" she says. "Because I got the best job!"

"Thanks, Miranda," I answer, with a big boing!

She turns to Humphrey, who is peering out from his cage. "You too, Humphrey! I promise I'll be the greatest animal keeper ever!"

He answers with an encouraging "Squeak!"

Before she heads for the door, I see her check his cage door to make sure it's locked.

She is already a first-class animal keeper!

"Good job!" I tell her.

But I guess all she hears is "BOING!"

My Mission Begins

· · · · · · · · · · · · · · · · ·

I t's good to think outside of the swamp once in a while," Granny Greenleaf told the other young tads and me. "Like Sir Hiram Hopwell, the famed frog explorer." We all dreamed of being as adventurous as Sir Hiram. "He was as brave as they come, but he wasn't foolish," Granny explained. "He planned his expeditions carefully to make sure he didn't run into trouble. So use your heads, little tads, and try not to get into trouble in the first place!"

It's morning, and already there's big trouble in Room 26. And I mean BIG!

Humphrey is trapped in his cage . . . and I can't do a thing to help him! He looks as miserable as if he were in jail. And I bet he feels like he's in jail, too!

The furry guy has a secret way of opening the lock on his cage and getting out. I've seen him do it with my own big froggy eyes. Somehow, he always manages to get back in his cage before humans see him.

Until last night. He opened the lock and scurried over to squeak at me. He was pretty upset about something. I tried to warn him that it was time for Aldo to arrive to clean, but he waited a few seconds too long. Aldo found him on the table!

After he put Humphrey back in his cage, Aldo took a paper clip and bent it around the door so it couldn't swing open.

Poor Humphrey spent the whole night trying to unbend the paper clip with his paws and teeth, but it didn't work.

Worse yet, Aldo left a note for Mrs. Brisbane telling her all about what happened.

And now, in front of the whole class, Mrs. Brisbane is blaming Miranda for leaving Humphrey's cage door unlocked.

"BOING-BOING! BOING-BOING!" I try to tell her she's wrong.

Humphrey does too. "SQUEAK-SQUEAK-SQUEAK!"

Of course, nobody can understand us.

"But I *did* lock the cage," Miranda tells the teacher. "I remember."

I remember, too, but Mrs. Brisbane doesn't believe her!

She is very serious as she says that Miranda didn't do her job . . . and she tells her to switch jobs with Art.

I guess everybody makes a mistake now and then, but this time it isn't Miranda who is in the wrong. It's our teacher! When Miranda begins to cry, I feel as helpless as a turtle stuck in its shell. Only, I am a frog stuck in a glass box, and I don't even have a door to jiggle open.

My mood improves a little bit when Mrs. Brisbane takes the paper clip off my neighbor's cage to check the lock. She sees that it's not broken—but Humphrey and I already knew that.

Despite her tears, Miranda manages to pull herself together and apologize to Mrs. Brisbane.

That was brave of her! It's not easy to say you're sorry when you did your best. But being brave means doing the right thing even if it's uncomfortable. I wonder if I could do what Miranda did.

One thing I've discovered about humans: They all make mistakes at one time or another. They're lucky, because if my friends in the swamp make a mistake, it usually means they meet an unfortunate end.

Mrs. Brisbane may not end up as a snapping turtle's supper, but she sure made a big mistake.

I'm hoppy that as the week continues, nobody mentions the cage door in class. Every afternoon, Mrs. Brisbane's students have been sharing their book reports, and today, it's A.J.'s turn.

"My book isn't a made-up story," he says. "Mine is all true."

"That's fine." Mrs. Brisbane nods. "That's called nonfiction."

"It's about as nonfiction as they come," A.J. says. "It's called *Tales of the Great Explorers*, and it tells the stories of real people who made great discoveries—lots of them."

I don't know anything about nonfiction or what that means, but I am interested in making discoveries. I wonder if there are any frog explorers in the book.

"Some of them traveled a long way over the sea, like Magellan and Balboa," he says. "And some traveled a long way over land, like Marco Polo and a guy named Louis Clark."

"They were two men," Mrs. Brisbane corrects him. "Lewis *and* Clark."

"That's them," A.J. says. "They explored all the western part of the United States when it was really wild."

I find this story *very* interesting. Almost as interesting as the stories Uncle Chinwag told about the famous frog adventurer, Sir Hiram Hopwell.

"Then there were explorers who went to outer space. They were astronauts who were launched in spaceships. Neil Armstrong was the first person ever to set foot on the moon." A.J. holds the book up to show a picture of a person on the moon.

This gets my blood pumping, because sometimes, when I start out with a huge leap, I feel as if *I'm* being launched into space.

"He said, 'One small step for man, one giant leap for mankind,'" A.J. continues.

He sure was a great leaper. Maybe Neil Armstrong was part frog!

"And did you come away from reading the book with some new ideas?" Mrs. Brisbane asks.

A.J. thinks for a moment. "At the end, the author says there are still places to explore and discover. I think that would be a cool job!"

Mrs. Brisbane chuckles. "Yes, indeed—if you like a challenge."

Heidi waves her hand wildly until the teacher calls on her.

"Aren't there any girl explorers?" She wrinkles her nose. "Were there only boys in the book?"

A.J. assures her there were girls. "Sure! There are women astronauts. And this one lady, she was the one who led that Louis Clark guy on his journey because she already knew where she was going."

"Then why can't we read about her?" Heidi wants to know. I think it's a good question.

"You can," Mrs. Brisbane says. "There are many good books in the library about female astronauts like Sally Ride, as well as Sacagawea, the Native American woman who guided Lewis and Clark. And you can look up some other explorers, like Amelia Earhart."

She glances at the clock. "Looks like it's time to announce who is taking Humphrey home this weekend," she says.

The room gets so quiet, you could hear a mosquito burp.

When Art is chosen, he looks as pleased as a green frog (me!) with a nice, fresh cricket!

⚶ ⚶ ⚶ ⚶

Once Humphrey is gone and the classroom is empty, it's time for me to get hop-hopping.

A.J.'s report about explorers has made me even more excited about my new mission to explore the human world. But to succeed, I'm going to have to figure out a way to get out of my tank.

Oh, yes, I can pop the top off. I've already done that a couple of times.

The problem is this: What happens once I'm out of the tank?

I need to focus, so I decide to take some time to Float. Doze. *Be.*

The gentle movement of the water helps me think, and I realize there are three problems. First, if I do leave the tank, I will start to dry out after a while. Not right away, but it's always wise to stay a little damp.

Also, I can pop the top of my tank and get out onto the table, but how do I get back *into* my tank? It's not as simple as walking through a cage door.

Finally, even if I figure out solutions to the first two problems, how do I safely get off the tabletop and into the broader world . . . and back again?

All this thinking has made me tired, but it takes a long time to fall asleep in the dark silence. In the swamp, night is my most awake time. I miss the sounds of owl hoots, bat wings flapping, singing crickets and the occasional scream of a red fox in the woods. (Well, maybe I don't miss that last one.)

I drift off, and when I wake up, sunbeams are dancing across the table. I take that to be a good sign.

It's the perfect day to start my new quest to explore the human world!

I do some warm-up leaps, preparing for the big moment when I pop the top of my tank. My goal is to move it just enough to make room to get out without knocking the top completely off. I work out how many jumps it will take.

Then I go for a quick dip, to make sure I'm as damp as I can be.

Ten, nine, eight, seven, six, five, four, three, two, one, and I have liftoff! If only Jumpin' Jack could see me!

After a nice, soft landing on the sack of Humphrey's

favorite snack, Nutri-Nibbles, I slide down and hop over to the edge of the table. I look down.

It's a lot farther than a hop, skip and a jump, believe me. Humphrey slides down the table leg to get to the floor. Then he swings his way back up using the blinds' cord.

I could probably manage both the table leg and the swinging if I happened to be a tree frog, which I am not. (Don't even get me started on those guys. Tiny frogs with their heads in the clouds. I prefer my feet near the ground, thank you!)

Tree frogs' toes are as sticky as glue, but my toes are only a little sticky, so I couldn't walk down the table leg like them. If I tried sliding the way Humphrey does, I'd probably have a very bumpy ride. Or tumble right off and land on my head.

Next, I examine the blinds' cord.

It's long and is made up of two slender ropes. Near the bottom, they are tied together, forming a little U shape.

I stare hard at that cord, trying to figure out if I can do anything with it. Humphrey uses it to get back up to our table. He grabs the cord with both paws, wraps his tiny toes around it and swings back and forth. Each time it goes a little higher.

Then—BING-BANG-BOING!—he lets go of the cord and leaps onto the tabletop!

It's incredibly brave of him.

Or incredibly dumb. Sometimes it's hard to tell the difference between brave and dumb.

I'm sure Louie the Loudmouth thought he was being brave and smart when he rum-rummed loudly at a passing group of ducks to ruffle their feathers. But because he wasn't paying attention, a long-legged crane swooped down and carried Louie away.

I'll bet the ducks quacked up about that!

I'm trying not to do anything too brave or too dumb, but something just right.

If I can't grasp the table leg, I can't grasp the cord, either.

I stare at that little U-shaped spot some more. It reminds me of a chair. Frogs don't sit in chairs, of course, but I think I could fit in it. But how would I get there in the first place?

I look down over the edge of the table again.

I don't think I'm brave enough to try it. Or maybe I'm not dumb enough. Either way, I'm going to have to think about how to get down there very carefully.

I climb up the bag of Nutri-Nibbles and dive back into my tank. At least the glass box is safe, and the water feels good on my skin as I splash around.

As I drift in the water, I think of a new verse for my song.

Rock-a-bye gently,
All through the night.
Have I solved the problem?
I must say not quite.

When I awaken
And morning is here,
I hope that the answer
Will become clear!

The next morning, I stare at the top of my tank. It is still open from my escape yesterday.

If I do manage to conquer the problem of the cord, I don't want my teacher and classmates to realize that I'm escaping my glass box.

But how in the swamp can I put the top back into position?

It's a good thing I'm an exceptional leaper: For most of the morning, I leap up and tap the top again and again. Each time, it moves a tiny bit.

Using the trial-and-error method, I tap it here, tap it there, until eventually it settles back into place.

It's still a little crooked, but maybe no one will notice.

I think Granny Greenleaf would be pleased, too. After all, she's the one who taught me, "If at first you don't succeed, leap, leap again."

I still have time for a nice doze, so I'm all rested up when Humphrey and the rest of my friends in Room 26 return from the weekend.

My furry neighbor seems excited to see me. I wish I

could understand what he's squeaking about, but Art seems happy, so I think he and Humphrey had a good weekend.

When Paul comes in the room for math class, something is different.

Usually, Paul hurries to his seat and never says a word—not even to me!

But today, he seems more relaxed. When he passes by Art's desk, they bump fists and Paul whispers something in Art's ear.

And they describe how Humphrey took an exciting train ride. I thought he went to Art's house. Did Paul end up there, too? And *what* train ride? Where did the little guy go?

All I can tell is that a big change took place over the weekend—Art and Paul are now friends. And Humphrey had something to do with it.

No time to think about that now because Mrs. Brisbane announces a pop math quiz. I didn't see this one coming. I hope the big tads don't pop *their* tops!

Paul quickly whizzes through the answers, while Art just stares at the paper. When he finally picks up his pencil, I can tell he's having a rough time, but he finishes the quiz.

It takes Mrs. Brisbane all the lunch period and then some to mark the tests. Humphrey stares at her and nibbles his toes. He's as nervous as a mouse passing by the spooky owl tree at midnight. And there's nothing more dangerous than *that*!

I slip into the water and drift until I hear Mrs. Brisbane announce that she is finished.

I can see by Art's smiling face that he did better than he expected.

Mandy got an F. An F should be a good thing! It could even stand for *Frog*. But the F makes Mandy look as unhappy as a long-necked crane with a sore throat.

"I can't believe I failed," she mumbles.

So that's it. F is for *Failed*.

Mrs. Brisbane tells her she can take the test again. If she passes *and* if she brings in a paper signed by her parents, she can take Humphrey home for the weekend.

Everybody always wants to take Humphrey home for the weekend, but so far, Mrs. Brisbane is the only human who has taken me home.

I wonder if *that* will ever change.

The Great Unknown
. . . .

I loved old Uncle Chinwag's tales of olden days in the swamp and about green frogs who had ventured to the Great Unknown outside of McKenzie's Marsh. Most of those stories don't have hoppy endings, though, because the explorer was never seen again! All except for Sir Hiram Hopwell . . . who always returned to share his exploits. I loved those tales of adventure, but I never thought I'd go to the Great Unknown myself. Or that the Great Unknown would be a school!

Miranda is sad that she lost her animal keeper job. Mandy is worried about her F. And I still haven't explored one bit of the human world. So, what will the rest of the week bring?

Things start out well, as Humphreyville is beginning to look like a real town.

But things turn sour when Mrs. Brisbane suggests that Paul help Mandy with her math so she can improve her test scores.

I hear Mandy mutter something about Paul being a know-it-all *and* being a baby! I'm not even sure how you can be both.

Art rushes to Paul's defense. "He is not!" he tells Mandy.

"Why would you say such a cruel thing?" the teacher asks.

Mandy hangs her head as she says she's sorry.

And then Mandy admits the truth. "I guess . . . Paul's so smart, he makes me feel . . . dumb."

"You are not dumb, Mandy. No one in this class is dumb," Mrs. Brisbane says.

Mandy is miserable. But *dumb*? Dumb is an owl that doesn't give a hoot, or a young frog who leaps before looking. Or a fish who thinks a worm will slide right off a hook.

Mandy is not dumb. And she proves it by agreeing to let Paul coach her on her math. Smart move!

When Jumpin' Jack and I were young frogs back in the swamp, he used to win every single leaping contest. I wasn't holding my head high then! One day, Jack pointed out that when I was midair, I wasn't stretching out my back legs as far as I could. I listened, and I practiced. Soon I could beat him at least half the time, but he didn't mind. He said it was more fun that way.

I think of Jack as I watch Paul sitting next to Mandy, patiently explaining how to solve the problem. Mandy nods her head a lot.

I guess she really listens, because after working with Paul, she gets a B on her next test! The B is for *Better* and for *Believing in Herself.*

The B makes her smile and makes me jump for joy.

Humphrey and I cheer with squeaks and boings, and Paul finally holds his head high.

Just before he leaves to return to Miss Loomis's class, Mandy reaches her hand into her backpack.

"Paul . . . I have something for you," she says.

"What is it?" he asks.

"*What is it?*" I boing.

Mandy stares down at her desk. "Nothing."

Paul looks confused. He starts to leave again, and I have to do something. "BOING-BOING-BOING!" I shout, hopping up and down on my rock.

Mandy turns her head to glance at me.

"What *is* it?" Paul asks. "Og and I want to know."

She reaches into her backpack again. This time she pulls something out. "I just made something to say thanks for your help," she mumbles as she hands it to him.

Paul stares down at the object. "Wow. Thank you! Did you really make it? For me?"

Mandy nods. "I like to make things. It's a bookmark, because I know you like to read."

Paul studies the bookmark carefully. "Thanks! I like all the colors and how you looped the yarn through the hole so it will hang out of a book."

Now Paul and Mandy look as happy as I feel.

Before the end of the day on Friday, Mrs. Brisbane announces that Mandy will be taking Humphrey home for the weekend. This time, she remembered to get the permission paper signed by her parents!

She doesn't look unhappy anymore.

But I glance over at Humphrey and see him gazing at Miranda: His whiskers are drooping. I think he still feels guilty for getting Miranda in trouble.

And I feel guilty because I don't have any idea how to help.

🐾 🐾 🐾 🐾

At the end of the day, Mandy's father and her little brother come to pick up Humphrey.

Mrs. Brisbane feeds me and tells me good-bye. "I guess you'll have a nice quiet weekend," she says. "See you Monday!"

I look forward to being by myself. I'll have plenty of time to work out the problem of how to see more of the school. If I can get around the way Humphrey does, I can do some real exploring!

But no matter how much I think about it, I can't figure it out. I wish Paul could help *me*. Or someone like Sacagawea.

I take some off time to Float. Doze. *Be.*

A few hours later, the door to Room 26 opens. I'm expecting Aldo, of course, so I am as rattled as a rattlesnake when I see Mr. Morales enter. He's the number one human at Longfellow School!

And he's not alone. He has a girl and a boy with him, and he's carrying a big box.

"Where is he, Dad?" the girl asks.

Aha! I've just learned something new. In addition to a whole school full of children to look after, our principal has young tads of his own.

"Over there, by the window," he says as he turns on the lights.

"I see him!" the boy exclaims, and rushes over to my tank. "Hi, Og the Frog!"

I answer with a "BOING-BOING," and the children squeal with laughter.

I hop up and down on my rock and try to act friendly. "BOING-BOING!" I repeat.

The children hop up and down and try to imitate my twangy voice. "Boing! Boing! Boing! Boing! Boing!"

"Settle down, Willy," Mr. Morales says. "Stop jumping, Brenda."

The girl, Brenda, is quite the hopper! Willy is a little bit smaller than Brenda. And Brenda is a little bit smaller than the big tads in Room 26.

Mr. Morales leans in close to my tank. "Og, how would you like to have an adventure this weekend?"

"Adventure!" I shout. "Just what I've been looking for!" At last, it's my chance to learn more about the human world.

"You're coming home with us for the weekend!" Brenda says, jumping some more. With each hop she adds a boing.

"The whole weekend!" Willy adds. "Boing-boing! Boing-boing!"

I love to hop, but watching them makes me dizzy.

Mr. Morales gently sets my tank in the box, which has newspaper in it for padding.

"Don't worry, Og," he tells me. "Mrs. Brisbane told me exactly what to do to take good care of you."

Suddenly, everything goes black. Did one of the children turn out the lights?

Mr. Morales's voice is muffled as he says, "Sorry it's so dark, Og, but I put a quilt over the box to keep you warm."

"That's very thoughtful," I say.

I spend quite a while in the dark, being jostled and bounced up and down.

It's not easy peasy, but I try to stay calm. When we had heavy rain in the swamp, Granny Greenleaf used to say, "When there's a storm, stay calm and warm. That's the way to escape harm."

I can tell I'm riding in a car by the bumps in the road. I have only been in a car a few times, but it feels nothing like swimming in my tank.

There are so many waves, I feel a little bit seasick.

The car finally stops after a while. I can hear Brenda and Willy through the quilt.

"I'll carry him."

"No, *I'll* carry him."

"I'm older."

"So what?"

Then there's Mr. Morales's strong voice. "*I* will carry him. Now, go on into the house."

There's more bumping and thumping, and Mr. Morales says, "Let's put him here on the coffee table where you can get a good look at him."

Once my tank is out of the box, I can see I'm on a low table in a cozy living room with Brenda and Willy's four eyes staring at me intently.

I stare back.

"Let's play with him!" Without warning, Brenda takes the top off my tank.

"Whoa—stop!" Mr. Morales's voice is loud and clear.

Brenda freezes in place.

"Don't grab him," he says. "Frogs don't like to be handled."

"Thank you!" I say.

Maybe Mr. Morales is starting to understand me, because he says, "You're welcome!"

He takes a folded sheet of paper from his shirt pocket. "I took notes on everything Mrs. Brisbane told me about how to care for Señor Og."

He glances at the paper. "It says if you grab him by surprise, he might pee on you."

"Not on purpose!" I quickly explain. "BOING-*BOING*!!"

If I peed on a human on purpose, I'd be lower than a catfish. A catfish feeds off the *bottom* of the pond, and that's as low as you can get.

But something happens when I'm squeezed by surprise. I guess Mother Nature made it work that way, but I do pee . . . a little bit.

In a way, I wish humans didn't take it personally, but they do get the message.

"Eww! That's gross!" Brenda says.

Willy chuckles. "I think it's funny."

"*Respect*," Mr. Morales says. "You must respect other creatures, their habits and their feelings."

I respect Mr. Morales, and so do my classmates. I'm glad to know he respects me.

A woman hurries into the room. "I thought I'd never get off that call! But now I'm all ready for my appointment," she says. Then she sees my tank and stops. "Oh, here's our little visitor!"

"His name is Og," Willy says, grabbing the woman's arm. "Come see, Mom. He's a frog!"

He pulls her toward the tank, and she studies me for a moment. "He's a good-looking frog," she says.

Leave it to Mr. Morales to have a smart wife!

Mrs. Morales says to me, "I wish I could spend more time with you, Og. But I have to show houses all day tomorrow, and I'm hosting an open house on Sunday."

"That's how real estate goes," Mr. Morales says. "We'll fill you in on everything."

"I'll take care of Og!" Brenda says.

"Me! Me! *I'll* take care of Og," Willy shouts.

"You're too little," Brenda says.

"Am not!" Willy answers.

Mr. Morales claps his hands over his ears. "Enough! You're going to scare poor Og."

He doesn't realize that a little noise doesn't scare me. Especially after my life in the buzzy, boing-y, howling swamp.

I am hoppy that Brenda and Willy both want to take care of me, but I don't think Granny Greenleaf would approve of their behavior. Especially since their dad is such an important person. A principal!

Mrs. Morales rushes out the door. "See you later!" she says.

Just then, Mr. Morales's phone rings. He says, "Hello,"

then covers the phone and tells his children that it's an important call and he must take it.

"Please quietly watch Og," he tells them.

Brenda pulls a small chair up close to my tank and sits. Willy pulls a small chair even closer to my tank and sits.

They are watching me the way humans stare at their televisions. What do they think this is? A TV show?

It's boring sitting in a glass box with four eyes fixed on me, so I slide off my rock and paddle in the water.

"Ooh—look!" Brenda says.

Willy giggles.

The water feels great on my skin, so I swim in a circle, adding in some extra splashing.

"Wow, look! He's swimming!" Willy says.

"Of course he swims," Brenda tells him. "He's a frog. Don't you know *anything*?"

Finally, I float. I don't move a muscle.

There is silence.

"Is he okay?" Willy wants to know.

"I don't know," Brenda answers. "Maybe he . . ."

"Maybe he croaked!" Willy shouts.

That does it. I start swimming again to show that I have no plans to croak!

"He's awesome," Brenda says.

That's better. I hop back onto my rock.

"Do something else, Og," Willy begs.

"I am not a trained dog who does tricks," I tell him. "I'm a wild, exploring frog."

"Boinnnng! Boinnnng!" they chime in together, howling with laughter. "Boing-boing-boing-boing!"

Mr. Morales rushes in, holding the phone to his ear. "Shush, *niños*! I'm on the phone!"

They lower their howls to soft giggles. Then they sit and stare at me again.

"What do we do next?" Willy whispers loudly.

Brenda shrugs. They are quiet until Brenda leaps up and, with a smile, rushes to a bookcase.

"I'll read him my favorite story! I know he'll like it," she says.

I think I'll like it. No one has ever read a story just for me before.

"You don't have to read to me," Willy says. "*I* can read."

"Not a hard book like this." Brenda settles back down in the chair with the book. "Og, this is a fairy tale," she says.

Willy groans. "Fairy tale? Yuck! Why would *he* like a fairy tale?"

"Because . . . it's about a *frog*!" Brenda says.

Somebody wrote a story about a frog? I'm all ears. (Even if you can't see mine.)

"The name of this story is 'The Frog Prince,'" she announces.

A frog that's a prince? I think I will like this story a *lot*.

All Hail Prince Boing-Boing

According to Uncle Chinwag, it was a sunny day when Sir Hiram Hopwell first boldly leaped into the Great Unknown. "I will miss the swamp," he announced. "But unless someone explores the Great Unknown, we will all live in darkness and fear." Darkness and fear aren't good, but BING-BANG-BOING, could I ever be brave enough to take that first step?

"Once upon a time—" Brenda begins reading.

Willy crosses his arms and wrinkles his nose. "Why do fairy tales all begin the same way? 'Once upon a time.'"

Brenda ignores him. "Once upon a time, there was a beautiful princess, who lived in a mag ... magni ... magnificent castle."

"I thought this was about a prince," I say.

Willy giggles and points to me. "He's Prince Boing-Boing," he says.

Brenda ignores him and continues reading about how beautiful the princess was. Willy moans, but I am interested. I wish Brenda would show me a picture of the princess.

Brenda reads the story with a lot of feeling. One day, the princess was playing with her favorite toy—a golden ball—when it fell into a well. She cried about her missing toy until a voice asked her what was wrong. The voice seemed to be coming from the well. She looked down and saw a frog! This surprises me because I never heard of a frog living in a well.

"I will get the ball for you," the frog said.

For some reason, the human princess could understand this frog. I wish my human friends could understand *me*.

"In return for bringing you the ball, you must agree that I will live in your palace, eat delicious food from your golden plates, drink from your golden cups and sleep on your beautiful, soft pillow," the frog told her.

"And you will return the ball to me?" she asked. "Then of course!"

The frog believed her and dove down to retrieve the ball.

The princess took it, and then—here's the bad part of the story—she ran off!

That princess was not nice! She made a promise, and she didn't keep it. As Granny Greenleaf often said, "Break a promise, and I fear, you'll be sorry throughout the year."

This not-nice princess was not one bit sorry! She returned to her magnificent castle and all her golden toys.

But that night after dinner, as she climbed the stairs to her room, guess who was there to meet her? Yep, one upset frog.

I like this part of the story because this is not a frog who gives up easily, and neither am I. He jumped out of the well *and* figured out how to get all the way into a castle. And he made a lot of noise when he demanded all the things she promised.

The princess argued with him, and when her dad, the king, overheard them, he showed up and asked what was going on.

I end up liking the king a lot because, like Granny Greenleaf, he told her if she made a promise, she had to honor it. "I command it!" he said.

His daughter wasn't happy about this (because she was a not-very-nice princess), but her dad was the king, and she did what he said. She took the frog into her room, gave him delicious food and drink and let him sleep on her beautiful, soft pillow.

I'm thinking that if someone treated me the way *she* treated that frog, I would hop out of there as soon as possible. But not that frog!

Then—another twist! Right before she blew out her bedside candle that night, the frog asked her to kiss him good night.

Personally, I don't think I'd like a human's puffy pink lips on my skin, but it turned out this frog knew what he was doing.

When the princess gave him a teeny tiny kiss, the frog turned into a handsome *human* prince—just like that!

I don't know who made up this story, but it's full of surprises! It turns out a witch in a bad mood put a curse on the prince, turned him into a frog and threw him into the well. That makes her even *worse* than the not-so-nice princess.

The princess was much more interested in the frog then. Not only because he was a handsome human, but because he had his own beautiful castle in his own personal kingdom. So they went off and got married!

"And they lived happily ever after," Brenda reads at the end.

Now I understand why the frog asked her to kiss him, but I'm not so sure I understand why he wanted to *marry* her. Maybe living in a well for a long time clouded his thinking.

In the end, I'm hoppy they lived happily ever after.

"That story doesn't make sense," Willy argues. "Who'd want to marry a princess like her?"

Willy and I think alike.

"You don't understand," Brenda tells him. She seems thrilled by the ending. "Og might be a handsome prince!"

Willy makes a face. "Handsome?"

42

I'm not sure if I'm a prince, but I am good-looking for a frog. Even Mrs. Morales said so.

"Did you like the story, Og?" Brenda asks me.

"Not bad," I say. "I liked the part about him having his own kingdom."

"Boing-boing to you," Willy says.

Brenda sighs. "Og should have his own castle."

Willy giggles. "He's not really a prince. That's just a story."

Brenda leans in and stares at me intently. "He could be. *You* can't tell."

Even though I don't agree with her about how good the story is, she could be right. Maybe I *am* a prince. That's what the frognapper said.

Brenda stares at me intently. "What would a frog castle look like?" she wonders.

Willy thinks. "It would be small and muddy."

"No way. Castles are supposed to be big!" his sister says. "And don't forget, Og is a prince."

"You are *loco*," Willy says. "He's *not* a prince."

Brenda answers, "I think he is."

Snakes alive! I don't know what to think!

"We need to build Prince Boing-Boing a castle," Brenda says.

Willy isn't interested. "Who cares about some old prince, anyway? He sits in a castle all day. Big deal."

"You don't know anything about princes," Brenda insists. "Princes explore new lands and go on quests! They face dragons and giants and have sword fights."

"They do?" Suddenly, Willy looks interested. "That's cool."

I'm interested, too. Exploring is what I'm yearning for!

Brenda hands Willy her book and tells him to look at the pictures.

"Wow, this giant has one eye in the middle of his forehead!" he exclaims.

I wish I could look at those pictures.

"But Og *has* to have a castle," Brenda says. "I'll draw a picture of it."

Before you can say "catch a cricket," she takes out paper and crayons and is drawing as fast as a hungry snapping turtle chasing a toad.

"Frogs live in swamps. I saw it on TV," Willy says. "They like places that are damp and muddy. So he'd have a swampy castle."

Wow—I like the way he thinks.

"No, no, no!" Brenda insists. "If he's a prince, his castle should be big and beautiful, with sparkles."

Willy shakes his head. "He's a frog. It should be muddy. No sparkles."

Nobody asks me what *I* think, but I'd prefer the muddy castle.

Soon, Willy is drawing, too.

After a while, Mr. Morales reappears. "Wow, it's nice to see you two working quietly together."

He comes up to my tank. "Señor Og, I think you are a good influence."

"Thank you," I reply.

"But we need to have dinner," he says. "Mom's clients want to put in an offer on a house, so she has to stay longer. Are you two up for our famous *tacos Morales*?"

Brenda and Willy jump up and down, shouting, "Yay!"

"Let's go make them," he says.

Soon they are off in the kitchen. I am hoppy for the break. I need time to think about that story and about being a prince.

What if a swamp witch put a curse on me when I was a tiny tad and I don't remember? I never saw any dragons or one-eyed giants in the swamp, but if I had my own kingdom, I bet I could stop the bullying bullfrogs from making so much noise.

I could ban snapping turtles and water moccasins completely.

I could make the decisions.

I float in the water and try to imagine such a life.

Mrs. Morales returns home in time to eat tacos with the rest of the family. Afterward, they all come in to check on me.

"So, Og, I hear that you are a prince," Mrs. Morales says. "*El principe.*"

In Spanish, it almost sounds like "principal."

Willy and Brenda show their parents their drawings.

"Wow, such different takes on his castle," Mr. Morales says.

"I'm impressed with them both," his wife says. "You kids are so creative."

"*Mine* looks more like a castle," Brenda says.

Willy doesn't agree. "Not for a frog!"

"Show them to me," I boing. "I want to see my castles!"

They laugh at my boings, then move into another room to watch a movie. I can hear the tads on the way.

"I want to watch the princess movie," Brenda says.

"Aw, I don't want to see that," Willy complains.

Brenda explains that it has a prince in it, too.

"And a giant?" Willy asks.

"Nope. A fire-breathing dragon!" she tells him.

Willy happily agrees to watch.

Meanwhile, I'm left alone on the coffee table. And the drawings are on the sofa on the other side of the room.

I am curious about those drawings. After all, one of those castles might be a nice future home for me. Is it big? Is it mucky? Are there crickets nearby?

After the movie, Brenda and Willy rush in to tell me good night.

"Can I kiss him?" Brenda asks. "And see if he turns into a handsome prince?"

I'm curious about that myself. (*Not* the kissing part. Just the handsome-prince part.)

"No kissing, except your mom and dad," Mr. Morales says, and he whisks them out of the room.

I must admit, I am relieved.

Slowly, the house gets quiet. Willy and Brenda must be asleep. I hear the voices of their parents for a while, and then the house is dark and silent.

There's a little light coming from the hallway, so I can see the sofa across the room.

I sure would like to see those castle drawings. Because maybe I am a prince! I mean, who knows? I'm almost starting to believe it.

And somehow, a song starts to grow in my brain.

I'm a prince!
I'm a prince!
Brave as can be!
Brave as can be!
I love to go on a daring quest.
I hardly even get time to rest.
They say as a prince I'm the very best.
Oh, I'm a prince!

I'm a prince!
I'm a prince!
All hail to me!
All hail to me!
I'd love to live a most princely life,
With a beautiful princess for a wife,
A life of leisure, with little strife!
Oh, I'm a prince!

I Leap Outside the Box

. . . .

According to the legend, the Great Unknown wasn't anything like the swamp. Some places had tall mountains reaching up to the clouds. Others had roads, with humans riding creatures with large hooves. (Sir Hiram kept clear of them.) The worst was the flat kingdom as dry as dust, with no green to speak of except tall plants with scary needles. Sir Hiram was in big trouble there! He hopped his way to a far-off tree that had dew on the bark and got as much water as he could to keep going. When night fell, he hopped like a jittery jackrabbit until he got to a woodsy, damp place. Whew—safety at last!

In Room 26, there's no safe way for a frog to get down off the table, because it's so tall. But here in the principal's house, my tank is on a low table.

It's so low, I could probably pop the top off my tank, leap

49

onto the table, drop down onto the carpet below and hop on over to the sofa where the drawings are.

But how would I get up on the sofa? Right now, I wish I could be as good at climbing as a tree frog.

The sofa isn't too high, however, and right next to it is a low, padded footstool. It looks like a bouncy toadstool to me. And maybe—just maybe—that might be the key to getting up to the sofa.

However, I can't explore new territory without first leaving my tank.

I decide to pop the top.

I focus on one corner and begin to leap. All that leaping-hopping-swimming practice on the weekends is paying off. I am a lean, mean froggy machine!

After six or eight good leaps, the top moves enough to create a space big enough for me to leap through safely.

And BING-BANG-*BOING*—I make it, landing squarely on the tabletop.

I stop to catch my breath and then take a short hop down to the footstool. It's as fuzzy and springy as the mossy shore of a pond.

I start slowly. Small bounce. Bigger bounce. Aim-high bounce. Go-for-it bounce!

Using the combination of the springy footstool and my powerful back legs, I launch myself through the air. Wheee! Did Neil Armstrong feel so free when he headed to the moon?

Touchdown! I land on the nice, soft sofa, right next to a soft pillow.

Welcome to Planet Sofa!

It does feel like another world. The sofa is so cushy, I sink down with every step. And it's so dry that my toes stick to the cloth a little bit. I wonder if Sir Hiram Hopwell's explorations were ever like this!

I make my way to the drawings and stand back to study them.

The two castles couldn't be more different. The first picture shows a tall, narrow one with whirly towers and a little stream of water around it. I like the water part. I'm not so crazy about the green walls. I'm also not sure how I'd ever hop to the top.

The little starbursts? I guess those are sparkles.

I like the flag on top of the castle with a picture of a green frog on it. Next to it is a second flag that reads PRINCE BOING-BOING'S CASTLE.

The other drawing is a mound of something muddy and messy that makes me homesick for the swamp. I can almost smell the muckiness of it. This building also has a stream around it, and it's shaped to look *something* like a castle, if you use your imagination.

It has a flag on top that says KINGDOM OF OG—KEEP OUT—THAT MEANS YOU!

I'm pretty sure that the green castle is Brenda's drawing and the other one is Willy's.

And since I love a damp and mucky home, Willy's is just about perfect.

I know one thing: It was worth all that effort to get out of my tank to see these. I'm glad I took the risk!

I know something else: Getting back to my tank may be more difficult than getting over here. But if I'm going to be a prince, I must be the bravest in my kingdom. I must try, even when it's hard. Now I have to get to the table.

I take a deep breath. Remembering Granny Greenleaf's advice, I look before I leap and take the plunge from the sofa to the footstool. Now I have to get to the table.

It's not that far, but the timing must be perfect.

Again, I begin with small bounces, working my way up to big ones. Keeping my eyes on my target (the table), I take another deep breath. "That's one small hop for a frog and one giant leap for frogkind!" I say as I take flight and soar through the air. I feel as light as a butterfly and almost as graceful.

I land on the table, but not nearly as gracefully as a butterfly. I didn't think about the smooth table being so slick, and I slip and do a series of somersaults. There's no way to put on the brakes . . . but incredibly, I stop short of sailing off the edge.

I pause there for a moment to catch my breath. Then it's time to go back inside the tank.

Whoa! I forgot to have a plan for this move. Leaping out of the tank was hard enough. Leaping back *in* will be more dangerous. There is no bag of Nutri-Nibbles to help me get part of the way.

I could miss completely and sail off the table.

Or I could have a hard landing or end up hitting the corner of the tank.

"If you stop your rushing and your hurrying, you'll have to do a lot less worrying." That's one of Granny Greenleaf's favorite sayings. It sounds like good advice to me.

I take my time. I hop around the tank first, to find the best place to begin my jump through the opening.

In my journey around the tank, I notice a couple of crayon boxes on the table. I hop onto them, and I'm much closer to the top of the tank now.

I remind myself how powerful my legs are. How often I outjumped all my froggy friends—except for Jumpin' Jack. He kept me on my toes!

This one's for you, Jack, I think as I leap up over the edge of the tank, land on a mossy spot on my rock and—oops!— slide straight into the water. It's a bit of a shock, but the water feels wet and wonderful.

I made it!

Even though I'm tired, I swim a few victory laps, all the while humming:

I'm a prince!
I'm a prince!

See how I swim!
See how I swim!
My legs are powerful, that is true.
I've practiced as much as a frog can do.
I set a goal, and I followed through.
Oh, I'm a prince!

Then I climb up on my rock, and I quickly fall asleep.

Back in the swamp, I woke up to some incredible noises—splashing, howling, flapping, the cawing of crows.

But in the Morales home, I'm awakened by loud shrieks. They're annoying, but not particularly dangerous.

"Hi, Og!!! Did you sleep okay?" Brenda yells.

"Og! Og! Og! What a frog! Frog! Frog!!" Willy shouts.

Mrs. Morales hurries through the living room toward the front door, followed by her husband. "Gymnastics for Brenda at ten o'clock. Soccer for Willy at eleven. Pick Brenda up and take her to her clarinet lesson. After the game, pick up Willy, then Brenda. Got it?"

"Yes," Mr. Morales says with a big yawn. "And then drop Willy at Max's house and take Brenda to the mall to get shoes before picking Willy up at five."

After she's gone, the rest of the family disappears to another part of the house. A little later, they scramble out the front door.

"See you later, Og!" Mr. Morales says.

"Bye!" Brenda and Willy shout.

And then they're gone. I stare at Planet Sofa for a while, then launch into my weekend exercise routine.

It's dark outside and I'm dozing when the door opens again and Brenda and Willy race across the room.

"Did you miss us?" Brenda asks. "Because I really missed you! Oh—watch me do a backbend!"

I must admit, it is amazing to watch her bend her body backward and touch her hands to the floor.

"Og, you should see me kick a goal. Pow!" Willy tells me, kicking at the air.

"It's just *baby* soccer," Brenda says.

"I'm not a baby!" Willy says. "Take that back!"

"*Silencio, niños!*" Mr. Morales says, sticking his fingers in his ears.

Luckily, Mrs. Morales comes home and the argument ends. "Let's go out for pizza," she says. "And celebrate . . . because I sold a house!"

Everybody cheers, and in an instant, they are all out the door and I am alone again.

Living with the Morales family is like living in a busy beehive, only slightly noisier.

Now I have plenty of time to relax and Float. Doze. *Be.* Then I go to sleep.

The next morning, the whirlwind of activity begins again.

"Good morning, dear little Og," Brenda greets me.

"Hiya, Og!" Willy says as he races into the room. "How's my favorite frog?"

I'm glad I'm his favorite. But if he could turn the volume down a notch, I'd appreciate it.

I slide into the water, where the noise is muted but I can still hear them.

"Today we're building your castle!" Willy says. "One that looks like my picture!"

"No way," Brenda says. "We're building the castle *I* drew!"

Willy demands to know, "Why yours?"

"Because I'm older and I know more. And you're the baby of the family."

"*BABY?*" Willy shouts. "*I AM NOT A BABY!!!*"

Then I hear a familiar voice. "*Niños*, I don't think you're building either castle. At least not today," Mr. Morales says.

His children wail, "Noooo!"

"Today is cousin Diego's birthday party—don't you remember? There's going to be a magician and a piñata, *musica*, good food and games! Doesn't that sound like fun?" Mr. Morales says.

Brenda and Willy nod their heads, but they aren't smiling.

I don't know what all those things are, but it doesn't sound as if there will be any *frogs* invited to the party.

Back in the swamp, our hatchday celebrations were

simple but tons of fun. Many of us shared the same hatch-day, which made it even more fun. We had leaping contests and lily pad racing. And then everyone gathered around and sang to the guests of honor.

> Happy hatchday to you.
> Happy hatchday to you.
> We're so happy you're here,
> Happy hatchday to you.
> (And many more!)

Frogs have big families, so we sang that song a lot!

"Can we take Og to the party?" Willy asks.

That boy thinks like me!

"No, I don't think it would be a safe place for him," his dad answers.

Since when does a brave prince have to worry about safety?

"Then when are we going to build his castle?" Brenda asks.

I like that girl!

Mr. Morales thinks for a moment. "I can ask Mrs. Brisbane if we can bring him home again next weekend," he says.

Brenda and Willy jump up and down so much, waves start to form in my tank water.

"YAY!!!!!" they shout.

"YAY!!!!" I agree.

"But she could say no," Mr. Morales warns us.

I hope Mrs. Brisbane agrees, because I'm starting to like the idea of having a castle a lot.

Once the family has gone off to the party, I think about looking at those drawings again, but to tell the truth, it wasn't so easy peasy to get to that sofa and back.

I take the well-known advice Uncle Chinwag gave me back in the swamp.

Float. Doze. Be.

And you will live so happily.

I have a hoppy day, even without magicians, piñatas and games.

But I must admit, I'm kind of bothered by the way Brenda treats Willy. He may be younger than her, but he's a smart young tad with good ideas. I've gotten a lot of good ideas by listening to all kinds of creatures. After all, it's Humphrey (a rodent) who inspired my wish to get out of my tank and explore.

I wish I could explain that to Brenda, but my boings aren't enough. There must be another way!

Trouble in Humphreyville

"Did Sir Hiram ever meet frogs like us?" I asked once. Uncle Chinwag nodded. "Yes, many times. He met green frogs, and frogs that were blue, yellow, striped and spotted. There were frogs of all sizes. Some had horns, some had hair, and some were poisonous! But most of them were downright nice and helped him survive the strange places he visited. Except, of course, for the bullying bullfrogs!"

Mr. Morales takes me back to school very early. He's a hard worker. I guess that's one reason he's the principal!

"You were a good guest," he tells me. "I hope you'll visit again next weekend," he says as he leaves me on the table.

"Me too!" I reply.

Mrs. Brisbane comes in early, too.

"Good morning, Og." She peeks in my cage. "Looks like the Morales family took good care of you."

"Of course," I say. "BOING-BOING."

Then the big tads come in, and Mr. Payne carries Humphrey back to our table. Mandy is at his side.

"Come back soon, Humphrey," she says. *"Please!"*

Later, when there's less commotion, I ask Humphrey about his weekend.

"SQUEAK-SQUEAK-SQUEAK!" He sounds excited when he answers.

I wish there was a way for me to tell him about the castle drawings, but there's not. And he probably has no idea that I might be a prince.

But I try to talk to him anyway, because that's what friends do.

"BOING-BOING! BOING-BOING!" I explain.

"SQUEAK? SQUEAK? SQUEAK?"

I still can't understand him, but at least we're both trying.

The morning starts off with a BING-BANG-BOING as Mrs. Brisbane announces that all the big tads' families will be coming next week to see Humphreyville when it's completed.

Great! I'll get to meet a lot of humans at one time and see what they're like.

Then Mrs. Brisbane assigns jobs for the week.

Miranda looks sad when Gail is named the new animal keeper. And I don't blame her, since it wasn't her fault that Humphrey got out of his cage. He looks unhappy, too.

When Paul comes in, Mandy suggests that he should have a job. Even if he only comes to class for math, he's part of Room 26. Art backs her up.

Mrs. Brisbane agrees and makes Paul the class accountant. That's a great choice, as he will be good at adding up the points the big tads are earning with their jobs.

Except for Miranda's situation, everything runs smoothly in Room 26.

Monday goes so well, I look forward to Tuesday, but am shocked when Mandy, Art and Heidi don't show up for school. Three big tads are absent on one day—that has not happened since I've been in Room 26! Where could they be?

When the rest of the big tads are at lunch, Mr. Morales comes in to talk to Mrs. Brisbane.

"Hi, Mr. Morales!" I boing at him, but he doesn't seem to notice.

He doesn't even smile when he greets Mrs. Brisbane.

I think something is very wrong.

Unfortunately, I am right. Mr. Morales has had a complaint from a parent . . . about Humphrey.

"SQUEAK?" my neighbor shrieks.

I am speechless. Or boingless.

"Apparently Mandy and her whole family are sick.

Coughs, runny nose, watery eyes. And Mrs. Payne blames it all on Humphrey," he explains.

"No way!" I protest.

"Humphrey!" Mrs. Brisbane exclaims. "Why on earth would she think that?"

That's what I want to know!

"Well, he spent the weekend at their house, and now they're all sick." Mr. Morales shakes his head. Then he says that Mrs. Payne has been calling some of the other parents. "She even threatened to start a petition to get all classroom pets banned!"

Snakes alive! I'm a classroom pet. Am *I* going to be banned, too? Am I going to have to move back to the swamp just as I'm beginning to explore? I still have lots more to learn. As sad as I was to leave, I'm not ready to go back now!

When I glance over at Humphrey's cage to see if he's listening, his whiskers are drooping and he's squeakless for the first time since I've known him.

Humphrey and I aren't the only ones who are upset. Mrs. Brisbane is fuming, and Mr. Morales looks miserable. They decide to do research to see if other students at school have gotten sick after handling classroom pets.

And Mr. Morales suggests that Mrs. Brisbane take Humphrey *and* me to her house for a while.

I like going to visit the Brisbanes' house. But I don't think I'd like being *banned from school*. Especially for something I didn't do!

While Mrs. Brisbane packs up our food after school, Sayeh stops to say good-bye. "It isn't right," she says in her soft voice. "They're our classroom pets. They're important. We named a whole town after Humphrey!"

"They'll be back," Mrs. Brisbane tells her.

I'm not sure . . . and when I look over at Humphrey, he looks even smaller than usual.

꙳ ꙳ ꙳ ꙳

Mr. Brisbane gives Humphrey and me a warm welcome. He comes out to the car to greet us in his wheelchair and carries my tank on his lap. It's a nice, smooth ride.

I'm hoppy to find out that he's on the side of us classroom pets! Once Humphrey and I are settled in the house, Mrs. Brisbane gets on the phone calling the big tads' parents.

After each call, she tells her husband, Bert, what was said.

Art's mom says her son has a bad cold, but her husband had it first. "Everyone in his office has it," says Mrs. Brisbane.

"See? Humphrey didn't make the Payne family sick," I say.

"SQUEAK-SQUEAK-SQUEAK!" my friend responds. He sounds as relieved as I am.

Mrs. Brisbane calls Heidi's house next, but Humphrey didn't even *stay* there. Her mom says Heidi has a bad cough.

I'm as jumpy as a jackrabbit when Mrs. Brisbane

decides to phone Mrs. Payne. Even Bert agrees that she's a troublemaker.

But when Mrs. Brisbane calls, she talks to *Mr.* Payne. It turns out that his wife works at night.

Humphrey tries and tries to tell the Brisbanes something. He squeaks his tiny lungs out.

"SQUEAK-SQUEAK-SQUEAK!" he repeats over and over, but they can't figure out what he's saying. Neither can I, but I think I can guess.

Later, Mr. and Mrs. Brisbane make a little maze for Humphrey to run. It cheers me up to watch the little guy cleverly racing past all the obstacles. I think it perks him up, too.

While we're watching him, Aldo calls. He was worried when he came to clean Room 26 and Humphrey and I weren't there.

Good old Aldo. It's nice to be missed. I miss him, too.

Even though I'm upset about everything I've seen today, when Mr. Brisbane feeds me a cricket, I relax . . . a little.

Humphrey and I are both on edge the next day, especially after Mrs. Brisbane leaves for school. It doesn't feel right to think of Room 26 without us there.

It's so quiet here, I think it's the perfect time to Float. Doze. *Be.*

But it's not easy to *Be* when you have an excitable hamster pacing back and forth in his cage all day.

I love the Brisbanes, but this is not what I had in mind when I decided to explore uncharted territory. Where's my big adventure? The way things are going, I'll never become a legend like Sir Hiram Hopwell.

Humphrey heads into his hut for a nap, so I let my mind roam free, and suddenly, I'm humming a little tune.

I've been yearning for adventure,
All the livelong day!
I've been yearning for adventure,
How I long to get away!
I could scale the highest mountain,
I could swim the deep blue sea,
I could have a great adventure,
An explorer I could be!

I would like to roam,
I would like to roam,
I would like to roam so far away!
I would like to roam,
I would like to roam,
I would like to roam today!

Mr. Brisbane is busy in other rooms of the house for

most of the day, until he decides to clean Humphrey's cage. That's when he makes a shocking discovery.

"Humphrey . . . I don't think you've been eating your food. You've been hiding it!" he says.

I'm upset at that news, too. Usually, Humphrey is as hungry as an owl who's had bad luck all week.

I wonder if a juicy cricket would improve his appetite. Probably not.

"If you don't eat, you'll get sick," Mr. Brisbane says. And when he thinks about it, he wonders if Humphrey *is* sick.

"Why didn't we think of this sooner?" he says. "You need to see a veterinarian!"

I have no idea what that is, but when Mrs. Brisbane gets home and talks to her husband, I figure out that a veterinarian, or a vet, is a doctor for animals.

I keep a close eye on my furry neighbor, who looks unhappy, worried and thin.

When they whisk Humphrey away for his appointment, I feel a little bit sick myself . . . from worry.

What if there *is* something wrong with the little fellow? And what if he's banned from Room 26 forever?

That would disappoint the big tads. And it would leave me as their only classroom pet!

Until now, I've been hoppy to let Humphrey do the toughest jobs. He has a knack for figuring out the big tads' problems and how to solve them. How would I manage?

Truthfully, I'm not sure I am up to it. Not yet.

While the Brisbanes and Humphrey are gone, I try to Float. Doze. *Be.*

But how can you relax when your best friend might be sick?

At last the door opens and Bert Brisbane rolls in with Humphrey's cage on his lap. Mrs. Brisbane is right behind him with the biggest smile on her face.

"Og!" she calls. "Humphrey's fine! He's completely healthy!"

"SQUEAK-SQUEAK-SQUEAK-SQUEAK-SQUEAK!" Humphrey adds.

"Tell Mrs. Payne that!" I suggest loudly.

"Bert, I'm so glad Mr. Payne and Mandy met us there," Mrs. Brisbane says. "It was good for them to see for themselves that Humphrey's not sick."

I hope that Mr. Payne will tell Mrs. Payne what the vet said.

Once Humphrey's settled back on the table, Mrs. Brisbane brings him all kinds of good things to eat: an apple slice, some raisins and some of his favorite yogurt drops.

Humphrey gobbles them all up. He doesn't even bother to store them in his cheek pouches!

He *looks* better, too!

"I guess it's back to school for the two of you," Bert says to Humphrey and me. "I'll miss you here, though."

"I think Humphrey should stay here tomorrow," his wife says. "He can rest and eat normally. Og can go back, since he was never at Mandy's house, but I want to show Mr. Morales and Mrs. Payne the veterinarian's report before I bring Humphrey back."

I'm hoppy to hear that I'm returning to Room 26. But without Humphrey? That takes some of the hop out of my hoppiness.

Right before I doze off late that night, I remember the time Granny Greenleaf appointed Jumpin' Jack spokesfrog for the green frogs. He was chosen to present a request from us to the bullfrogs for some quiet time every day.

Jack was nervous, but Granny Greenleaf said, "Put your mind to it, and you can do it."

I'm nervous about being the only classroom pet in Room 26 tomorrow. I'm not like Humphrey at all, and I haven't been in school for very long. But I'm going to put my mind to it and try to be helpful in my own way.

I hope I'm more successful than Jack, because the truth is, the bullfrogs only got noisier. But then, as we know from Sir Hiram Hopwell, bullfrogs are like that everywhere.

On the Job

Once, Sir Hiram Hopwell stayed too long up north in the Great Unknown. He fell fast asleep when the temperatures dipped. It was a long, long winter, but one day, a loud cracking noise woke him. The ice was breaking up! Sir Hiram couldn't wait to get back to his family and friends. He quickly hopped onto a large ice block, but as he floated south, the ice began to melt. He was riding a tiny sliver of ice when he heard a roaring sound. He was heading for a steep waterfall! Sir Hiram had the adventure of his life whooshing down a mountain in that waterfall, and he made it back to the swamp. Now, that's a hero!

"Where's Humphrey?" A.J. asks loudly on Thursday morning when he sees that I am the only classroom pet around.

Heidi gasps. "Did something happen to Humphrey? Where is he?"

"He's fine, calm down," Mrs. Brisbane tells them. "He's at my house, and the veterinarian said he's completely healthy."

The big tads relax a little, but Garth asks, "Then why is Og here and Humphrey isn't?"

I wonder if Mrs. Brisbane is going to say, "Because Mandy's mom raised a big fuss over nothing."

She does not. After all, this whole mess isn't Mandy's fault. Maybe it's not anybody's fault.

"Humphrey will be back as soon as Mr. Morales gives the okay," our teacher says. "I gave him the vet's report this morning. Meanwhile, my husband is happy to have him at home today."

Sayeh glances toward my tank and looks worried. "Won't Og be lonely without Humphrey?"

Mrs. Brisbane smiles. "He probably will. But we'll keep him busy."

I miss him already. I miss the squeaky voice. I miss the screechy wheel. Most of all, I miss having such a lively neighbor.

But I can't sit here feeling sorry for myself, because I have work to do. One thing I've noticed about Humphrey is that he constantly watches and listens to everything that goes on in the classroom.

I do that, too, but sometimes my mind drifts. But today, I'm as alert as a hungry hawk circling the swamp. I'm determined not to miss a thing.

When Paul comes in for math class, the first thing he says is "Hi, Og!" But he glances over at the spot where Humphrey's cage usually sits and adds, "Where's Humphrey?"

Mrs. Brisbane explains, and Paul seems satisfied, but he doesn't budge.

"I believe it's rare for humans to get illnesses from pets," he says. "I'm not sure about hamsters, but I can do some research on that."

Mrs. Brisbane nods. "That would be helpful, Paul."

He lingers by my tank and then he asks a question. "Excuse me, but when was the last time Og's tank was cleaned?"

"I think Miss Loomis cleaned it before Og moved to our classroom," Mrs. Brisbane says.

I keep my mouth shut, but I know that Miss Loomis didn't.

Paul sniffs. And he sniffs again. "There's kind of a smell," he says.

That's funny, because I don't smell anything.

Mrs. Brisbane joins Paul next to our table and sniffs. "It does smell a little . . . *swampy*," she says.

What's wrong with that? Nothing says "home" like a nice, swampy smell!

"The tank probably needs cleaning," Paul says. "Every month or two it needs cleaning, because frogs shed skin—"

"Ewww!" was the cry from the big tads.

Paul shrugs. "It's just natural, but in a tank, germs can start growing."

"Oh, dear," Mrs. Brisbane says. "That's not good."

Truthfully, I have no idea what they're talking about, although I now realize that the view from my tank isn't exactly clear.

"Do you know how to clean a tank?" Mrs. Brisbane asks.

"I have a general idea," Paul says. "But I can find out the exact steps to follow." He glances around Room 26. "You'll need a big sink."

Mrs. Brisbane nods. "I understand. Thank you, Paul. You do the research. I'll try to set something up, and you can be in charge."

"Don't I have anything to say about this?" I ask.

The big tads laugh.

Mrs. Brisbane changes the subject to math, and Paul takes his seat.

While the rest of the class concentrates on numbers, I concentrate on *them*.

At first, things seem normal. Even a little bit boring. I wouldn't mind a nice nap, but then I notice something.

Seth drops his pencil.

He picks it up and then noisily scoots his chair back from the table.

"Hey, you rocked the table!" Heidi objects.

"Sorry," Seth says, running his hand through his hair several times.

Mrs. Brisbane continues with the class, and I keep on watching Seth. It isn't long before he starts jiggling his feet.

"Seth, sit still, please," Mrs. Brisbane tells him.

"Sorry," he says. But before long, he's drumming his fingers on the table. It sounds like a woodpecker on a busy day.

"Shhh!" Mandy hushes him.

He stops drumming, but a few seconds later, he is back at it again.

"Seth!" Mrs. Brisbane says. "I'm trying to teach here. And it would help both of us if you'd be still."

Seth runs his hands through his hair again. "Sorry," he mumbles.

Now I can see that Seth is trying not to fidget, but he's not succeeding!

No matter how many times his friends shush him or Mrs. Brisbane asks him to settle down or he says he's sorry, Seth keeps moving and making noise.

Everyone—including Seth and the teacher—seems relieved when the bell rings for recess.

"Seth, could I talk to you before you go?" Mrs. Brisbane asks as the students stream out the door.

When they're alone, Mrs. Brisbane says, "You've been much better at sitting still lately. But today—well, any idea why you're having so much trouble?"

Seth shifts from one foot to the other, looking miserable. "I don't know," he says. "I guess I do better when Humphrey is here."

Everybody does better when Humphrey is here, especially me!

"How so?" Mrs. Brisbane asks.

Seth rubs his eyes and then scratches his neck. "When I'm feeling kind of jumpy, I stare at Humphrey's cage and I settle down. I figured that out when Humphrey was at my house."

"I see," the teacher says. "So doing that helps you focus?"

"I guess so," Seth answers. "Anyway, it works. Unless he's not here."

Mrs. Brisbane nods. "I think that's a good start. But maybe there are other things that could help you focus. Taking a few long, deep breaths. Taking notes. Or . . ." She glances over at my tank. "Maybe you could concentrate on Og. He's pretty interesting, too."

Aw, I'm so glad she noticed!

Seth says, "I think he's awesome with that long tongue and green skin."

"Let's see if Og thinks he can help." Mrs. Brisbane leads Seth over to my tank.

I'll tell you what I think: I think it's a great idea!

"Hi, Og!" Seth greets me with a big, bright smile.

"Hi, Seth! BOING-BOING!" I answer.

"I sure like the sound he makes," Seth says.

"There's nothing like it," our teacher agrees. "But he generally stays quiet during class."

Seth nods. "That's true."

"I think he saves his moving-around time for after class," Mrs. Brisbane adds.

She's been paying more attention to me than I thought!

"You probably don't know this, Seth, but at recess time, Og swims and leaps and splashes around. Then he's calm during class."

Mrs. Brisbane is right as usual. Does she know all my secrets?

But since Humphrey isn't here to help, I'm going to try. I plunge into the water and splash like crazy. Then I leap up onto my rock and do some jumping jacks.

"Wow, look at him go!" Seth exclaims.

Mrs. Brisbane nods. "Yes, I wish I could do that. How about you, Seth? How are you at jumping jacks?"

The boy immediately launches into an amazing series of peppy jumps, waving his arms at the same time. He may not be quite up to the standards of Jack and me, but he's only got human legs to work with.

Seth finally stops to catch his breath.

"Feeling better?" Mrs. Brisbane asks. She has a huge smile on her face. I like her best when she smiles like that.

"I do," Seth answers. "But I can't get up and do jumping jacks in class."

"But if you do jumping jacks and all kinds of active exercises at recess, it might help you be calmer in class," she suggests.

"BING-BANG-BOING!" I pop up and agree, and they both laugh.

"I'm going to go out and do jumping jacks right now!" Seth says, heading for the door.

"Don't forget your jacket," Mrs. Brisbane reminds him.

After Seth has raced out the door, the teacher turns to me and says, "Thank you, Og. You are a real help to the class. We need you more than ever now."

Then she leaves the classroom while I catch my breath.

"BING-BANG-BOING!" I repeat. I didn't know if I was up to it, but I helped the big tads all by myself. I'm feeling a little more confident. Granny Greenleaf would be proud.

I take a few moments to Float. Doze. *Be.* And I feel calm.

Once the big tads are back, they go to work on their town. "It feels strange to be working on Humphreyville when Humphrey's not here," Sayeh says.

"I know," Mrs. Brisbane replies. "But think how proud he'll be of the progress you make."

And I am proud of the progress *I've* made.

I celebrate by hopping onto my rock and then sliding back down into the water.

I'm not sure how long I've been floating and dozing when I suddenly hear Mrs. Brisbane say, "Gail! Could you tell us what is so fascinating about Og?"

There's a lot that's fascinating about me, but I think she's trying to get Gail to work on her project instead of staring at me.

"Og's been floating for a long time, and he hasn't moved a muscle. I think maybe he's sick. Or even . . . dead!"

I leap up at the word *dead* to assure Gail that I'm very much alive.

"He's fine, Gail," Mrs. Brisbane says. "He certainly looks healthy to me."

Strangely enough, Gail is still staring at my tank.

"Gail?" Mrs. Brisbane says.

"I'm sorry, Mrs. Brisbane, but Og gave me an idea," Gail says. A few seconds later, though, she mumbles, "Never mind," and returns to her table.

"I'd like to hear your idea. Why don't you share it with us?" the teacher asks. "Is it about Humphreyville?"

"Yes, but it's probably just silly," Gail says.

"*I'd* like to hear your idea!" I boing as I get back up on my rock and start hopping to encourage her.

Gail giggles, the way she always does.

"Tell us, Gail," Miranda says.

"Yeah," A.J. adds. "I'd like to hear your big idea."

"I think something is missing," she says. "Something important." For once, Gail looks very serious and doesn't giggle even once.

"What could be missing?" her friend Heidi asks. "We have a school and houses, city hall and even a hospital."

"For *people*," Gail says. "But what about the animals, like dogs and cats, hamsters and frogs? They get sick, too. We need somewhere for them to go when that happens."

77

She has a very good point.

"That's a great idea!" Sayeh says. Other students nod and agree.

"Will you lead the project, Gail?" Mrs. Brisbane says. "I happen to have a box left."

Gail hesitates. "I don't like being in charge. Maybe someone else can do it."

I understand. It's not easy peasy to be in charge.

"But I think you should try. After all, it's your idea," the teacher tells her.

"Everyone will help," Garth offers.

"Well . . . okay," Gail agrees, but she doesn't look happy about it.

"So where do we start?" Tabitha asks.

Gail thinks for a moment. "When I thought Og was sick, I remembered that Humphrey had to see the vet. In most animal hospitals, the animals are in plain cages, staring at bare walls," she says. "I'd like to make this one less scary, with lots of toys to play with, and windows so they can get fresh air and look at the grass and trees, and a pretty place to walk the dogs and cats outside as they get better."

The whole class gets to work, drawing, coloring and cutting things out.

"It should be a happy, colorful place," Gail says.

Mrs. Brisbane lets them work on it for the rest of the day.

When the bell's about to ring, the Humphreyville Pet Hospital is complete, surrounded by colorful paper trees and flowers. There are many windows, and each one has the face of an animal looking out: a dog, a cat, a hamster, a bird and a frog!

By the time everyone has admired it, Gail is her giggly self again.

"Thank you for your great idea, Gail," Mrs. Brisbane says. "After all, our animal friends are an important part of the community, too."

Gail looks so proud, I can't help boinging, "Way to go, Gail!"

I'd be proud, too. Even though she wasn't comfortable with being a leader, Gail gave it a try, and it worked out great! Sir Hiram Hopwell always thought outside the swamp . . . and *she* thought outside the box.

And who's to say I can't do that, too?

I'm all set to greet my little buddy Friday morning when Mrs. Brisbane comes in . . . *without* Humphrey and his cage!

My heart takes a few leaps until Mrs. Brisbane says, "Class, I have good news. Humphrey will be back here on Monday."

Everyone cheers . . . but no one cheers louder than I do.

I watch Seth carefully in class, and he seems calmer, especially after recess. And Gail grins as she passes the animal hospital on her way to her table. Excellent!

When Paul comes in for math, Mrs. Brisbane whispers

something to him that I can't hear. He nods and shows her a paper he's brought with him.

After math is finished, Paul usually goes back to Miss Loomis's class, but not today.

"Class, Paul has given me a detailed plan for cleaning Og's tank. And Mrs. Goldman is going to help us out. As you know, her art classroom has a large, deep sink for cleaning paintbrushes and such. A team of you, led by Paul, will be taking Og and his tank in there."

I am pleased to see every hand in class go up and start waving.

"Pick me," Gail begs.

"Please, let me do it," Garth says.

A.J. waves his arm and in his loud voice bellows, "Pick me, Paul!"

Paul glances at Mrs. Brisbane with a look of panic on his face. Luckily, our teacher already has a plan—as usual.

"Class, I've written each of your names on a strip of paper and put them in this bowl." She holds up a bowl, reaches inside and shows the class the strips of paper. "I'm going to have Paul close his eyes and pick out three names. They will be the helpers this time. And don't worry if you don't get selected. Og will need his tank cleaned out again."

Paul closes his eyes tightly, reaches into the bowl and, one by one, picks out three strips of paper.

Mrs. Brisbane reads out the names. "Miranda Golden."

Miranda looks thrilled! After being fired from her job as animal keeper, she is getting another chance.

"Garth Tugwell!" Mrs. Brisbane announces.

Garth beams.

"Mandy Payne!" she declares.

Mandy stands up and takes a bow. Everyone laughs.

Then, before I know it, my tank is placed on a cart and Paul wheels me out of the classroom and down the hall toward the art room, with Miranda, Garth and Mandy following behind.

I suddenly realize that I have no idea where we're going and what will happen there.

But it's okay . . . because maybe this is the great adventure I've been longing for. To the hallway . . . and beyond!

My Incredible Journey
. . . .

Sir Hiram Hopwell came back to the swamp to share his adventures in the Great Unknown with his green frog family. But I wondered about the explorers in Uncle Chinwag's stories who never returned. One day I asked him why they never came back to the swamp. He thought and then in his slow, sure way replied, "I like to think it's because they found exactly what they were looking for. Or something even better!" Jumpin' jackrabbits! I'd never imagined anything better than the swamp!

I'm excited, and I guess Paul is, too, because we are whizzing past lots of doors and classrooms. I even get a quick glimpse of what must be the playground where the big tads go for recess. Mandy, Miranda and Garth have a hard time keeping up. At last I feel as if I'm heading out on a great adventure! And I didn't have to slide down the table leg or figure out how to get under the door.

I feel as free as a frog floating on a lily pad, and I'm inspired by a new song floating around in my head.

Gone exploring,
Gone exploring,
Gone exploring for a while.
Hope I find what I am seeking,
Gone exploring for a while.

I am searching,
I am searching,
I am searching to find out
What this new world has to offer
And just what it's all about.

Keep on seeking,
Keep on seeking,
Keep on seeking every clue,
To discover all that's out there
And what humans really do!

Gone exploring,
Gone exploring,
Gone exploring for a while.
I am sure to find adventure,
Gone exploring for a while.

My song stops when Paul takes a sharp turn into a classroom. I see right away that it doesn't look anything like Room 26 or Miss Loomis's room.

Those are nice rooms, but they aren't nearly as colorful and sunny as this one. It's big with long tables and brightly colored stools with lots of students sitting on them. And so many colorful things on the walls!

I also see tubs and brushes. Boldly patterned drawers. This room almost has a life of its own. And then I see it: a deep, wide sink with faucets. What a lovely swimming hole that would make! Instead, that sink must be for cleaning my tank.

That's okay, I guess, but I wish I could be part of the class. I don't know a thing about art . . . but I want to learn!

Paul wheels my tank toward a woman at the front of the classroom. She is wearing a loose shirt with splatters of paint all over. Messy, but colorful.

Her hair is all gathered up on top of her head in a knot, and there's something bright and red sticking out of it. Is that a paintbrush?

Her lips are bright red, too.

"This must be Og! Welcome to art class!" she says, opening her arms wide. "You look like a work of art yourself! Thank you, Paul, for bringing Og here."

"BOING-BOING!" I greet her.

"Did you hear that, class?" she asks. "Og speaks a beautiful language!"

"BOING-BOING!" I thank her. If only she could *understand* my beautiful language.

She leans in close to my tank. "Aren't you a vibrant green? I would like to paint you."

I am not sure I'd like to have paint smeared all over me. I hope that's not what she has in mind.

"I am Mrs. Goldman. I'm not as colorful as you are, but at least I have a colorful name," she tells me.

I try to tell her I like her name, even if all she hears is "BOING-BOING!"

"Class, today Paul, Mandy, Miranda and Garth are going to be cleaning Og's tank in our big sink, and Paul will tell us about what he's doing," she explains. "While they are doing that, this is a good chance for us to work on color and shading. I think Og here would make an excellent model!"

I jump for joy. "BOING!" I am going to be part of art class!

There are a lot of giggles, and a few tads shout out, "Hi, Og!"

Then Paul takes over. And being Paul, he is very serious as he explains what they need to do.

"First, we all have to wash our hands." He turns on the water and swishes his hands around. "We won't use soap or chemicals, because they could irritate Og's skin," he says. "Just make sure you rinse them really well."

So far, so good. Irritated skin would make me as cranky

as a bear that stepped on a beehive! I'm so glad Paul knows what he's doing.

Mandy, Miranda and Garth take turns rinsing their hands.

"Of course, we must take Og out of his tank while we clean it," Paul says. He takes a bowl from the cart. "This temporary container is big enough so he can't hop out."

I don't say anything, but I think Paul underestimates my jumping ability.

Then Paul reaches into my tank and I brace myself. Even though he's moving nice and slow, I'm still a little nervous.

"Watch out!" Mandy says. "I picked him up once, and he peed on me!"

The students burst out laughing, but it's not funny. It's true! I couldn't help myself.

"I'll be careful." He slowly scoops me up and gently sets me in the bowl.

Miranda places a thin sheet of plastic over the top and Garth puts a rubber band around that. Paul quickly pokes some holes in the plastic. "For air," he says.

They *definitely* underestimate my jumping ability.

I'm disappointed that I've been moved from a box to a bowl. I'll bet Lewis and Clark and Sir Hiram Hopwell were never put into a bowl. At least I can see this new world of the art class counter through the glass.

"Class, I know you'd all like to see what's going on, so why don't you come up a few at a time to watch?" Mrs. Goldman says. "We'll start with your row, Rosie."

Four students make their way up to the sink, where Paul and the other big tads are taking everything out of my tank. All my plants, rocks, the gravel from the bottom—everything!

"Be careful!" I say.

The art students at the sink giggle.

"He sounds silly. Why does he say 'boing'?" one of the boys asks.

"That's the way green frogs talk," Paul says. "He is a green frog, but his scientific name is *Rana clamitans*."

Back in the swamp, all I knew was that I was a green frog called Bongo. I didn't know I was a *Rana clamitans* until I got to Room 26, but it sounds important. That Paul is one smart tad!

While Mandy, Miranda and Garth scrub all the items from my tank, I turn away because my bare tank is a sad sight to me.

But I'm cheered when the first group of tads turns to focus on me.

A girl with a huge smile rolls over in a chair on wheels, like Mr. Brisbane uses. "Hi, Og. Remember me? Rosie?"

"Of course I remember. Hi, Rosie!" I answer. She is in Miss Loomis's class.

"George is quieter now that you're gone, but I miss you," she says.

"I miss you, too! But I don't miss George!" I reply, remembering how that disagreeable bullfrog used to **RUM-RUM** at me day and night. Humphrey may be a bit squeaky, but he is not loud and rude.

As more students come up to view the tank cleaning, Paul patiently explains how he used special tablets to clean the water he'll be putting in my tank, how bits of food could pollute the water and how they must scrape off any dead skin I've shed.

Some more students come over to see me. I know a few others from Miss Loomis's class, like Harry, who is often late to class, and the girl with red hair, Kelsey.

"Hi, Og. Do you like your new class?" she asks.

"Yes, I do!" I answer. "I liked my old class, too, except for George."

Kelsey giggles. "Boing-boing to you, too!"

After the last group visits me, I figure out that half of the students are from Miss Loomis's class and half of them come from another classroom.

I glance over and see that Paul, Mandy, Miranda and Garth are still busy with my tank. If I'm going to go exploring, this is my chance!

While they're distracted, I make one huge bounding leap, and ta-da! The rubber band flies off and zooms toward the wall. Luckily, none of the big tads notice. I see a gap in the plastic on one side of the bowl, so I aim right for that spot and hop onto the counter.

Nobody notices that, either, and I quietly move forward into the Land of Art. And what a strange new land it is!

I pass a mountain of glue pots stacked on top of one another, and reach a colorful crayon fence. One big leap, and I'm over it! I'm making a lot of progress, and I don't even have Sacagawea to guide me.

Just as I head across a cardboard bridge, I hear Rosie's voice.

"Og has escaped!" she shouts.

There's a lot of commotion as the big tads rush forward, gasping and shrieking.

"I'll get him!" Paul says. "Stop, Og! Stop!"

Did Sir Hiram Hopwell stop halfway through his exploration? Never! And I certainly won't.

"Let's see what he does," Mrs. Goldman says in a calm voice.

"Watch it. He might leap off the edge," Paul warns.

"We'll make sure he doesn't," the teacher says.

She is giving me my freedom! No wonder I like her.

Paul is smart, but he doesn't realize how smart I am, and there's no way I'm going to leap off the counter and plunge to the floor!

I remember Granny Greenleaf saying, "Never leap unless you're sure you'll land in a safe place."

All eyes are on me as I move forward. I hop past a forest

of brushes of all sizes and colors. And then I do a series of leaps over the pink eraser hills.

Even though I've roamed far from McKenzie Marsh, I have never seen sights like these!

I've been out of my tank for a while now and I'm starting to feel dry, so I turn around and head back to the sink. The water is running, and it looks like a waterfall. We only had a waterfall in the swamp after a huge rain—and it was a tiny dribble.

This waterfall looks inviting and powerful, so I hurry toward it.

"Sorry, Og," Paul says. "The sink might be dangerous." Doesn't he realize that I know how to swim?

Boom! The bowl comes down over me like a dome.

I am busted! But I have taken a leap into a world that I'm pretty sure no other frog has seen before.

Paul turns the bowl right side up, and Miranda gently lifts me up and sets me inside. After Mandy pours in some of the treated water, Garth puts a thick book over the top, leaving a tiny gap for air.

I'm not going to try to pop *that* top.

Mrs. Goldman leans in close. "Og, you are a bold and beautiful frog," she says.

And she is one bold and beautiful teacher!

The excitement is over, and the students go back to their seats.

Then Mrs. Goldman leads a boy up to meet me. I hadn't noticed him before. But instead of looking at me, he looks down at his shoes.

"See, Charlie? It's a frog. And his name is Og," Mrs. Goldman says, but Charlie doesn't look up.

"Can you say hello to Charlie, Og?" she asks.

"Hi, Charlie!" I say. "BOING-BOING! BOING-BOING!"

My boings always make the big tads laugh, but not Charlie. He still won't look at me. I wonder what's so interesting about his shoes.

"Doesn't Og make a funny sound? I think he's being friendly," she says. "Let's say hello."

Charlie covers his ears.

He's about as friendly as a water moccasin. Or maybe he's shy, like a deer.

"Okay, Charlie. You can say hello to Og later," Mrs. Goldman says, and leads Charlie back to his table.

While Paul and his crew are putting my things back in the tank, Mrs. Goldman speaks to the class. "Since we're lucky enough to have Og in class today, let's try sketching him. Take out a piece of paper and your pencils, and we'll think about how to draw a frog," she says.

They all follow her instructions . . . except for Charlie. Now he stares at his tabletop. It doesn't look any more interesting than his shoes to me.

On a whiteboard, Mrs. Goldman starts demonstrating

different ways to draw a frog. I stop looking at Charlie and watch her instead.

It's fascinating to watch her make a few curved lines and some straight lines look like me!

She does a sideways drawing and a funny drawing of me looking straight on. She even adds a line that's my tongue catching a fly. Yum!

Then the students begin their own drawings. They work quietly, and I am surprised to see that Charlie is drawing something, too.

I try to hold still as they look up at me and then back to their papers.

"Mrs. Goldman, we're finished with the cleaning," Paul announces. "We need to put Og back in his tank."

"BOING!" I say. "Can't I have a little more time in the Land of Art? Please?"

"Yes, Paul, go ahead," Mrs. Goldman tells him.

I'm impressed how gentle Paul is with me. My tank feels different now, but I can see clearly through the glass. I can't say it smells different because it doesn't smell at all.

At least Miranda, Garth and Mandy have put everything back exactly where it belongs.

I still think about the swamp. It wasn't all sunbeams and butterflies there. There was danger all around. So even though there's no muck or mud in my tank, now it almost feels like home, sweet home, to me.

As Miranda rolls the cart with my tank on it out of the art room, Mrs. Goldman says, "I hope you'll bring Og back to model for us again soon, Paul."

"I will," he promises, and that's good news to me.

Mrs. Goldman suggests that the big tads say good-bye to me and leads them in a loud round of boings.

And a few seconds after that, I hear a strange, soft "boing!"

I glance back and see Charlie looking at me. Is he giving me a crooked little smile?

I think he likes me, and that makes me hoppy!

On the way back to Room 26, I add another verse to my song.

> Been exploring,
> Been exploring,
> Been exploring for a while.
> And I had a really good time,
> Plus I just made Charlie smile!

Paul smiles, too, when we get back to Room 26. My friends all want to come up and see my clean tank.

"Wow, how'd you know what to do?" A.J. asks him. "Have you got a frog?"

"No," Paul says. "But I read about it on the internet."

"It was a lot of work," Garth says. "But interesting."

"Can I help next time?" A.J. asks.

Richie, Heidi and Gail also beg to help.

"You'll all get a turn," Mrs. Brisbane says. I know why she's smiling. All the big tads now treat Paul like a member of the class.

I guess I had a part in that (and my dirty tank, too)!

Another Journey

· · · · · · · · · · · · · · · · ·

Granny Greenleaf liked to say, "There's no place like home, no matter where you roam. And don't forget, you might discover that what's out there is a lot worse than what's under your own nose!" But once an explorer gets started, he seems to keep on going. At least Sir Hiram Hopwell did. Lewis and Clark didn't give up, and once Neil Armstrong was headed to the moon, he kept on going. Once you take the first step, there's no turning back!

I've been so busy, I forget that it's Friday until mid-morning. This is the day Humphrey usually goes home with a student . . . but since he's not here, I guess he can't.

I make sure to keep my eyes and ears open to see what's happening in class, the way Humphrey would.

And what I see and hear surprises even me. "You want to come shoot some hoops with me this weekend?" Richie asks Paul.

Paul looks unsure and says he's not good at basketball.

"I'm not, either," Richie says. "It's just for fun."

Paul says he'll ask his mom. Then A.J. chimes in, "Can I come?"

And before long, Tabitha and Seth are planning to join Paul and his new friends, too. And no one looks happier about that than Paul. Except maybe me.

Shortly before the bell rings at the end of the day, Heidi blurts out a question. "Where is Humphrey spending the weekend?"

"At my house." Mrs. Brisbane smiles. "He's been with us so long, my husband is going to miss him when he comes back here on Monday."

"Well, we miss him *now*!" Heidi insists.

She is right. I miss him even more than I expected.

I wonder if he misses me?

Mrs. Brisbane glances at the clock. "Don't forget your math worksheets. And have a great weekend."

The bell rings and the students rush out.

As usual, Garth is the first to leave. He watches that clock like a hungry hawk.

Mrs. Brisbane hums a little as she straightens her desk. She's a tidy human. I don't think she'd like a mucky home.

Then she comes over to my tank. "Og, you were a big hit with Mr. Morales's children last weekend, and they'd like to have you back this weekend."

I bounce up and down on my rock. "Great!"

Maybe I can return to Planet Sofa . . . or maybe I will have my own castle!

"I thought you'd like that," she says. "He'll be picking you up soon. Oh, and your clean tank looks very spiffy!"

Spiffy? I'm not sure what that means, but since she's smiling, I think it must be something good.

Mrs. Brisbane puts on her coat and picks up her hand-bag. "Mr. Morales should be here any minute. He can let himself in."

I'm hoppy that I'm going off on another adventure. It was scary leaving the swamp, but now that I have, I want to keep exploring. I think of Sir Hiram, and I'm so inspired, a poem pops into my head.

A frog said farewell with a wave,
For adventure is what he did crave.
He went off on his own
To explore the unknown,
Oh, he was uncommonly brave!

It's not easy to start, it is true,
But take the first step, and then two,
Once you're out of the swamp
You may have a grand romp,
And you'll learn a great deal about you!

The door to Room 26 swings open, and there's the principal. "Sorry I'm late, Og," he says. "I had a meeting with some parents. But now I'm ready to take you home for the weekend. Brenda and Willy are so excited that you're coming, they're about to burst."

Sounds messy! But I bounce up and down on my rock. "I am, too!" I say.

And it's true. I haven't forgotten my last weekend at the Morales's house and the story of the frog prince.

I've been wondering all week what kind of prince I'd be. I'd like to be a dragon-finding, quest-taking, giant-fighter kind of prince and explore new lands!

"BOING-BOING!" I say. "Bring it on!"

It doesn't take long before my tank is bundled up in a quilt, and Mr. Morales hurries me out to the car.

I don't enjoy the bumpy ride, but I forget all about it when we get to the house and I hear Brenda and Willy.

"Og!!!!" they shriek.

"Quiet down, *niños*," their father says. "You'll scare poor Og."

They can't scare a brave prince like me, but my ears are vibrating like a hummingbird's wings.

Mr. Morales sets my tank on the low coffee table and removes the quilt. "So, what have you planned for our friend Og this weekend?" he asks his children.

Before they can answer, his phone buzzes. "Hello?" he says. "Hi, Dev. Yes, I can talk now . . ."

He waves at his children, points at the phone and leaves the room.

"The superintendent," Brenda says. I can tell from her tone of voice that although Mr. Morales is important at Longfellow School, the superintendent might be even a little *more* important.

"So, Og, here's the plan." Brenda kneels so she's looking straight into my tank. "We are going to build you a beautiful castle like my picture, and it will definitely be green."

"No way," Willy argues. "There's no such thing as a green castle."

"There is now," Brenda says.

Willy shakes his head. "I looked at a book about frogs in the library. Frogs like damp places and mostly live in muddy ponds or swamps."

Ah, yes—I do so love a mucky home!

"What are we going to make it out of?" Willy asks.

Brenda thinks. "Blocks or . . . I don't know . . . cardboard?"

"The book says frogs like dampness. And damp cardboard won't work," Willy says. "But we could use some mud and leaves and green stuff from the backyard."

"Ha!" Brenda says. "And where would we build it?"

"I was thinking . . . maybe in the bathtub," Willy explains.

Brenda is silent as she thinks about this. "But *Mom*. And *Dad*!"

"Oh, yeah." Willy stops and thinks. "Maybe they wouldn't understand."

When Mr. Morales returns, he looks worried. "The superintendent of schools wants me to draw up an emergency report by Monday, so I'll be here, but I'm going to be pretty busy," he says. "And Mom has houses to show tomorrow."

"It's okay," Willy says. "We can take care of ourselves."

Mr. Morales sits on a chair so he is eye to eye with his children. "Yes, *niños*, I know you can. But you two like to argue and bicker and try to push each other's buttons. And you know that's true."

Willy and Brenda look away and don't answer.

"I need you to get along this weekend," their dad continues. "Can you help your mom and me out?"

"Sure they can!" I answer.

All three of them burst out laughing.

"I take that 'boing' as a 'yes,'" Mr. Morales says.

"We'll try, Dad," Brenda says.

Willy nods.

Mr. Morales wraps his arms around them both. "*Gracias*," he says. "And you, too, Og."

"No *problema*!" I tell him.

"So, your father tells me you have a plan for Og this weekend," Mrs. Morales says when she gets home.

"We're building him a castle," Willy says.

His mother looks surprised, so Brenda adds, "Like in the story of the frog prince."

Mrs. Morales chuckles. "Well, Og *is* a prince of a frog!"

Remembering the frognapper's words, I answer, "BOING-BOING! That's what people keep saying."

But Mrs. Morales looks worried. "But can you two get along? If you can, I'll be very proud of you."

Brenda and Willy look at each other and nod, smiling.

I am not so sure.

After dinner, Mr. Morales sets up a board game in the other room, the one he calls a den. I think of a den as a place where skunks, foxes and other creatures live. But so far, the only nonhuman I've seen in the house is me!

The family disappears into their den for a few minutes, but then Mrs. Morales gets a phone call.

A few minutes later, Mr. Morales gets another call from the superintendent.

Brenda and Willy wander back into the living room, plop on the couch and stare at me for a while.

"I know what we need." Brenda smiles. "A princess for the frog to kiss . . . *after* he has his castle."

A real live princess to kiss me? I'm not so sure about *that*.

The lights are out, but I'm not sleeping. My mind is too full of princesses and castles . . . and the constant bickering between Brenda and Willy.

All evening, *she* sounds like the chorus of bullying bullfrogs. "RUM-RUM-RUM! I'm older and smarter than you are!"

He sounds like the complaining chorus of green frogs—and that includes me! For some reason, when the bullfrogs taunt us, we feel we must answer back. "BOING-BOING! We're smart, too. We can leap as high as you can!"

It goes on and on, and nothing ever changes.

I don't miss those battles of the frog families, not one bit. But I do want Brenda and Willy to stop arguing and build me a nice castle!

For now, it's time to Float. Doze. *Be.*

And in the morning, it'll be time to act!

I'm up early for a splashy swim and some jumping jacks to get my blood pumping.

Brenda greets me with a sweet smile. "Good morning, Prince Boing-Boing," she says.

"It sure is!" I reply.

When Willy joins her, she announces, "I'm going to start on my green castle."

Willy folds his arms. "And I'm going to make a mud castle. So there'll be two castles."

"Og will have to choose," Brenda says. "Of course, he'll choose *mine*."

She reminds me of someone back in the swamp—but who? Not Granny Greenleaf or Cousin Lucy Lou.

Then I start to think about Tammy Tad, one of my many, many big sisters. (I told you, frog families are large!) She thought that because she was older than I was, she was also smarter. That's the way Brenda feels about Willy.

Tammy always thought of me as a tadpole, even after I was a fully grown frog. And she liked to tell me how to do things.

"Wrap your tongue around that fly, or he'll get away," she'd remind me, even after I'd already caught the thing.

Or sometimes she'd say, "Grow up, Bongo!" And I was already grown-up.

When I was a little tad, her advice was helpful and welcome. When I was older, her advice was annoying.

All of that ended, however, on a nice breezy spring day when Tammy was floating on a lily pad, enjoying the warm sunshine.

I was splashing nearby when I noticed Chopper floating toward her lily pad. He looked a lot like a big rock, and I guess Tammy didn't notice his beady little eyes staring at her.

"Leap!" I shouted. "Tammy—leap! It's Chopper!"

Tammy was so shocked, she froze on that lily pad, and the snapping turtle floated closer.

"Leap! Swim! Do something!" I warned her, but she didn't budge.

I dived into the water and got directly beneath the lily pad. With my head on the bottom of the plant, I pushed it away from the snapping turtle as fast as I could.

Once we were close to shore, Tammy unfroze and hopped to dry ground. I swam out from under the lily pad and hightailed it up to the grass right behind her. We caught our breath inside a hollow log.

I was hoping Tammy would thank me, and she did. But what she said next was even more amazing. "Bongo, you saved my life. I guess you're not a little tad anymore. You're a brave grown-up frog."

She didn't boss me around after that, and we became good friends.

I wouldn't want Brenda to come face-to-face with a mean snapping turtle, but I sure would like her to see that Willy's not a baby anymore. They both have some good ideas—how can I get them to listen to each other?

That's a tall order for a medium-sized frog.

Granny Greenleaf would say, "When the time is right, don't be asleep. Grab the moment and take the leap!"

And I'll do it! But I need to figure out when the time is right.

A Frog's Home Is His Castle

. . . .

Sir Hiram Hopwell avoided humans as much as possible. But once, he was sunning himself near a lovely stream when a man surprised him. The man seemed harmless, until he scooped up Sir Hiram and took him to a castle . . . because he was a king! The king put Hiram in a lovely bowl of water and fed him his favorite bugs. But this was no life for an explorer. So Sir Hiram escaped the bowl, hopped past the guards, down the castle stairs and out the door, and swam across the moat. He was free to roam again!

Brenda and Willy get started on their castles right after breakfast. From my spot on the coffee table, I have a good view.

Willy makes many trips in and out the back door. He has

a pail that he seems to be filling with mud and then lugging to the bathroom. By his fourth trip, I wonder if there's any dirt left in the yard.

Brenda, on the other hand, works in her room. But after a while, she lugs a big box to the table where I am.

"Look, Og! I have everything that I need to build your castle." She puts the box on the table and pulls out small blocks of wood in different sizes and shapes.

"Okay, I'm starting with these." She stands up rectangular blocks side by side on the floor so they look like four walls with an opening in the front. There she places a square block with an opening and an arch on top.

"There's the door. But this is just the beginning," Brenda tells me. She starts stacking square blocks on the corners of the four walls. "See? These are the towers."

I don't quite see . . . yet.

On top of the rest of the wall, she places blocks that are notched across the top.

"And here are some windows for the towers." She adds some blocks with square openings in the middle to each corner.

Next, she makes the towers a little taller and puts smaller notched squares on top.

Brenda sits back to view her creation. "See? Now it's starting to look like a castle."

"I see," I boing. It does look a bit like a castle, if you use your imagination.

"Of course, it has to be green." She takes something out of the box. "Isn't this scarf pretty?"

It's light, and you can see through it, but it certainly is *green*.

"And you'll have a banner on top." She shows me a paper flag with PRINCE BOING-BOING'S CASTLE printed on it.

Next, Brenda pulls a jar of glittery things out of the box. "Plenty of bling! You *are* a prince, after all!"

Bling? Whatever that is, we don't have it in the swamp!

"It will be the perfect castle for a prince . . . and his princess," she adds.

About that princess . . . I wish I knew more about *her*.

I hear the back door slam again and then Willy's heavy footsteps on his way to the bathroom.

"You're making a mess!" Brenda calls to him.

Willy doesn't answer.

"This scarf will make the castle so comfy," she tells me. She places it over the castle and starts tucking it around the walls. "There. Now the outside will be all green . . . like you."

As she tucks the scarf around the last tower, it collapses into a heap.

"Ohhhh!" she moans.

"What's wrong?" Willy calls from the hallway.

Brenda says, "Nothing."

Willy appears in the doorway. I hardly recognize him because he looks like a toad that just hopped out of a mud puddle. He has dabs of mud on his face and hands and shoes.

He is also making a muddy mess on the floor. Don't get me wrong, I like muddy messes, but I don't think his parents will!

"Is *that* part of your castle?" he asks, pointing to the green heap.

"It will be," Brenda says. "I'm not finished."

"I'm glad to hear that," Willy mutters as he heads down the hall. "Because it looks like a big mess."

Brenda leaves the room and comes back with a roll of tape.

She rebuilds the walls and carefully begins to tape the scarf over them. She doesn't seem to notice that the windows and doors are hard to see. Instead, she hums happily as she sprinkles the bling, which turns out to be silver glitter, all over the castle.

Finally, she tapes her flag on the tallest tower.

She grins and claps her hands. "I did it!"

It doesn't look like a castle. It just looks like a sparkly green scarf.

"Don't get nervous," she tells me. "I'm going to pick you up so you can check out your castle. Please don't pee on me!"

"I'll do my best," I say.

I steel myself as she reaches into my tank, but she is gentle.

"Here you go, Prince Boing-Boing," she says as she places me on the top of one of the towers.

Right away, there's a problem. This scarf is sticking to my feet and won't let go, and the sparkles are scratchy. I want to tell her I'm uncomfortable, but all she'll hear is "BOING."

"Check it out, Og," Brenda says, prodding me with her finger. "Go on."

I try to move, but my toes stick to the scarf, and it starts clinging to the rest of my body, too. Including my mouth.

The scarf is drying out my skin. I need water—fast!

"Water!" I croak. I wiggle my toes free, take a giant leap off the tower onto the carpet and hop away as fast as I can toward the bathroom. I definitely heard the sound of running water in there. And maybe I can find out what Willy is doing with all that mud.

"Come back, Og!" Brenda shouts.

I'm sorry to upset her, but there's no time to waste!

In the bathroom, Willy is bent over the bathtub, focused on his work.

"BOING-BOING!" I say, hopping through the door. "I need water now!"

"Og!" Willy says. "Hey, you have to see your castle. You're going to love it!"

He bends down to pick me up. "Don't be scared. I won't hurt you."

"And I'll try not to pee on you," I promise.

I am good at keeping promises. Willy lifts me up to the edge of the tub.

I am expecting to see a castle. What I see is a total mess. There is mud everywhere, with a huge mound of dirt in the middle.

"Here's your castle, Prince Boing-Boing," Willy tells me. "See? Those are the towers."

I guess I can see two blobs of mud on either side of the big one.

"And the windows." He points to a line of square dents in the mud near the top of the blobs. "I tried to make them look fancy," he says, and I see that each "window" has a leaf in the center. I'm still not sure how you can see out of them, but they look nice.

"This is called the *moat*," he tells me, pointing to the muddy water encircling the castle. "You could use it as a swimming pool."

Now this castle is getting interesting!

"And here on the side, I made a giant water slide," Willy says. "See how I smoothed out the mud so you could go fast?"

I see what looks like a twisty road going down the side of the tallest tower.

"Want to try it?" he asks.

Do I want to try it? Do I want to slide in nice, damp mud and end up swimming in a pool? *BING-BANG-BOING!*

He gently sets me at the top of the slide, and—WHOOSH!—I am zipping down at a high speed as Willy cheers me on.

Suddenly, Brenda pokes her head in the doorway.

"Hey," she says, "Og's supposed to be trying out the castle I built for him."

"Watch this," Willy tells her. "Og loves his castle."

Brenda slowly approaches the tub. "Castle! It looks like a disgusting mess to me."

Willy sets me on top of the slide again. "Look at him go."

Wheee! I glide down the slide at top speed and—SPLASH! When I land in the water, I paddle like mad.

"Wow! Look at that!" she says. "That is cool!" Brenda sounds like she means it.

"Told you," Willy says.

He puts me back on top, and I take another wild ride.

The water in the moat feels amazing, especially after being so dry.

I swim around and around the castle, admiring it from every direction. Now I know how those great sea explorers like Magellan and Balboa must have felt when they sailed to faraway lands.

At last, I've gone where no frog has ever gone before!

Brenda picks me up and puts me on the slide. This time, I skip the ride down and dive directly into the water.

One giant leap for a frog!

Oops! When I land, I splash muddy water all over Brenda and Willy. Wet mud drips down their faces and onto their clothes, but they don't get mad. Instead, they howl with laughter.

I float around the moat. I haven't been so hoppy since the day I caught a fly and a cricket with one great swoop of my tongue.

I'm so hoppy, I sing.

How I love my floaty moat,
Floaty moat,
Floaty moat.
How I love my floaty moat,
One with a castle view.

I love to swim and make deep dives,
Make deep dives,
Make deep dives.
I love to swim and make deep dives.
I love my castle, too.

"Listen to that!" Brenda says. "It almost sounds like he's singing."

"Yeah. Og likes the castle, but I kind of wish it looked better," Willy admits.

Brenda nods. "I have some ideas. We could smooth out these towers."

She runs her hands over the muddy towers, and Willy helps. Then they mold notches on top with their fingers.

"And these windows? You need to make them alike." Brenda pokes deeper dents and centers the leaves in each one, and suddenly there are windows! Then she uses a twig to carve a wavy design around each one.

"That looks better," Willy says.

"I'm not finished," she says. "It needs a few more things."

She disappears, and I hope she's not bringing in the scarf and the glitter.

"Some bling," she says. I am hoppy to see that instead of glitter, she has brought small plastic flowers in all colors. She plants them in the mud outside the castle, and they look nice.

"How does it look?" Brenda asks. "Do you like it?"

Willy nods. "It looks a lot better."

"One more thing," Brenda says, and she plants the pink and green flag on top.

It's still a mucky mess . . . but it looks a whole lot more like a castle.

By now, I don't care *what* it looks like. I'm so happy for the mud and the water.

Willy and Brenda both smile as they admire their creation.

"WHAT ON EARTH IS GOING ON?" a voice yells.

They freeze.

"Dad!" Brenda whispers.

"Uh-oh," Willy says.

"I asked you to play nicely today. I did not ask you to make a mess!" he says as he enters the bathroom.

"Sorry, Dad. But look at how much Og likes his castle!" Willy says.

"It's the perfect castle for a frog prince," Brenda says.

Mr. Morales doesn't look at the castle. "Look at all this mud! The footprints on the floor—and the towels!"

"Sorry. But he loves it!" Brenda explains.

At last, her father looks down and sees me in my floaty moat. "And this is not healthy for Og. You aren't supposed to handle him and put him in mud! Mrs. Brisbane is going to be upset. And your mom is going to be *muy* upset."

I am *muy* upset that he can't see how hoppy I am.

To convince him, I start doing a backstroke around the moat, splashing happily. When I look up, Mr. Morales is still shaking his head, but he's also watching me.

"Watch this," Willy says. "I won't hurt him."

He picks me up gently and sets me down at the top of the slide.

The mud is nice and smooth from my previous trips. I shoot down the slide at record speed and land in the water with a gigantic splash.

"He looks pretty healthy to me," Brenda says.

Her dad looks surprised but then he starts laughing so hard, he can barely answer. "I have to admit, he does."

Soon, they're all laughing.

"You built this castle, Willy?" he asks.

"We both did," Willy says. "I started it, and then Brenda made it a lot better."

"It was Willy's idea," Brenda explains.

Mr. Morales is still smiling. "But now we must rinse Prince Boing-Boing off and put him back in his tank. And then clean up this mess."

"I'll do it, Dad," Willy promises.

"We'll do it," Brenda says.

She gently holds me under the faucet. The water feels so good, I relax, and—oops! Maybe a *little* pee escapes, but the water washes it away.

I am feeling content and hoppy until Brenda says, "Og, you are the prince of my dreams."

And then, without warning, she *kisses* the top of my head!

Her lips feel . . . strange. Dry and wet and . . . a little bit too human for me!

"BOING-BOING!" I am so shocked, I fly out of her hand and dive into the water again.

I don't want to kiss a princess! I don't want to kiss anyone. Blah! Eww! Yuck!

"Ick," Brenda says as she wipes her lips. "His skin is so . . . froggy."

"Brenda, go wash your face!" Mr. Morales says. "Willy,

put Og back in his tank *now*! And get rid of all this mud!"

"Can we at least take pictures of the castle first?" Brenda asks.

Mr. Morales gives in. He takes pictures of me swimming in the castle moat and another one of me going down the slide. Then he rinses me off again.

When he's finished, Mr. Morales says, "Now clean this mess up before your mother gets home!"

I keep track of the cleanup from the safety of my tank on the low table. Forget about roaming free. At least there's no chance of Brenda giving me another yucky kiss when I'm behind glass!

Willy makes many trips carrying buckets of mud back outside. Meanwhile, Brenda runs to the kitchen for more paper towels. "I've almost gotten rid of all the muddy fingerprints, Dad," I hear her tell her father.

By the time their mother gets home, I'm resting on my rock and have washed off all traces of human mouth germs. I've *almost* forgotten about the kiss.

Mrs. Morales is not happy to hear about the mess her children made while she was gone. But she *is* happy to see her children working together without complaint.

"Señor Og, I am glad you came to our house," Mrs. Morales tells me. "I was right. You are a prince of a frog!"

That's nice, but now I know that being a prince isn't all

it's cracked up to be—especially if it involves kissing! (But I'll bet even Sir Hiram Hopwell wasn't kissed by a princess.)

Even so, I'm glad that each of the Morales children could see that the other had a good idea. It wouldn't have been nearly as much fun without all the mud that Willy brought in. But it wouldn't have looked as much like a castle without Brenda's touches.

When things quiet down, I fall into a deep sleep. And for once, I don't even dream of the swamp.

But someone else in the house isn't sleeping tonight. Mr. Morales works at his desk for hours after the rest of the family goes to bed. His light is on almost all night.

The Trip to Humphreyville

. . . .

As a young tad, I dreamed of venturing out of the swamp myself. But I loved my life there, and my friends and family. I worried I would miss them if I left (and I do). Sometimes, I'd go to the very edge of the swamp and stare out at the Great Unknown. But I was too scared to take that one hop forward. I decided I wasn't brave enough to be an explorer like Sir Hiram. But it turns out I was toad-ally wrong!

Sunday at the Morales home is as busy as a beehive in a field of spring flowers. Mrs. Morales has work to do, and so does Mr. Morales. Brenda goes off to a playdate with her friend, and Willy goes to a ball game with his uncle.

I miss my castle, but I keep busy catching up with my exercise routine.

On Monday morning, I'm surprised that Mr. Morales is

the first person up and moving around. Especially after working late into the night.

"I'm going to school early to put the finishing touches on my plan," he tells his wife. "If you can get the kids to their school, I'll take Og back to Room Twenty-six."

The sun isn't even up yet as we head to Longfellow School. I feel as if I've been away for a long, long time and have gone far, far away.

We get to school so early, Mr. Morales must unlock the front door!

It is quiet in Room 26, so quiet that I can hear the clock slowly ticking away the minutes. The beginning of school is still hours away.

Plenty of time to Float. Doze. *Be.* That's when I do my best thinking.

My mission to explore the human world has gone well. I traveled across the Land of Art and Planet Sofa. I even took a fun journey to my own castle—with a floaty moat!

But I am still limited in what I can do . . . mainly because I can't get down to the floor and back the way Humphrey can. And that means I can't help my friends as much as he does.

I pop the top of my tank and land on the tabletop. Maybe I'll get a new idea.

Once again, my attention is on that little U-shaped place where the blinds' cords connect. The more I stare, the more that little U-shaped spot interests me. At first it reminded me of a chair. But now it reminds me of a swing. If I could sit there and start swinging—maybe I'd find a way to do what Humphrey does.

But frogs can't sit in little swings. And Humphrey only swings UP to the table. He slides DOWN, which is impossible for me.

I feel as helpless as a turtle without a shell. (Now, that's something I never saw and hope I never do.) I almost wish I could be a hamster instead of a frog. But I love being a frog!

And then—BING-BANG-*BOING*!—it dawns on me. I AM NOT A HAMSTER! All this time, I've been trying to think like Humphrey. But I'm a frog, and I think like a frog . . . and that's what makes me special.

And what does a frog do if he's in a difficult spot? He takes a leap! What makes us special is our amazing ability to jump. That's what our bodies—especially our legs—are made for.

I go to the edge of the table and look down. Now that I'm thinking like a frog, I see several places where I could leap. Right next to our table is a reading chair with a nice, soft cushion on it. And next to that is a low cabinet that has crayons and paper and other supplies in it. From there, the floor is a hop, skip and a jump away.

It's a challenge, but I've been exercising and have become an even better jumper than I was in the swamp.

It will be a giant leap for a frog . . . but I have to know if I'm brave enough.

"This is for you, Jack." I concentrate hard on the cushion on the chair. I will have to clear the arm, but I can do it.

Five . . . four . . . three . . . two . . . one—I go for it! My back legs propel me through space like Neil Armstrong's lunar module (that's what A.J. called it). And the frog has landed . . . right in the middle of the cushion!

A short hop to the cabinet is a no-brainer . . . as is the jump down to the ground. (Aldo does keep the floor amazingly dirt-free.)

I am looking forward to exploring the floor when I look up at the clock. Leapin' lizards—Mrs. Brisbane will be here any minute!

I hop back on the cabinet and jump to the chair. I pause on the cushion, because that leap UP to the table is twice as hard as the leap down. I imagine that Jumpin' Jack is beside me and we're having a contest, and I land safely.

I hear Mrs. Brisbane's key in the door as I hop up the good old Nutri-Nibbles bag and zoom back into my tank.

No time to get the top I popped back into place, but—BING-BANG-BOING!—I made it!

"Good morning, Og! Look who's here!" Mrs. Brisbane says. She hurries over to the table, carrying Humphrey's cage.

"Welcome back!" I tell my friend.

"SQUEAK-SQUEAK-SQUEAK!" Humphrey replies. I can tell he definitely missed me as much as I missed him.

Our teacher takes off her coat and gloves and straightens her desk before coming back over to my tank.

"Goodness, what happened here?" she wonders aloud. She pushes the top back into place. "Did you have a bumpy ride with Mr. Morales?"

She doesn't have time to think about it anymore, as the big tads are coming in the door.

I wasn't the only one who missed Humphrey. Every single big tad comes up to his cage to tell him that.

And I'm as hoppy as I ever was finding a cricket in a thicket when Seth tells Humphrey, "You should see the cool exercises I learned from Og while you were gone."

"SQUEAK!" my neighbor answers.

Then something amazing happens. Mrs. Brisbane makes an announcement. Sure, she makes announcements each morning, but this one is different.

"I want to tell you about a mistake I made," she says.

The big tads are completely silent. Even Seth doesn't move a muscle.

She tells the class she made a mistake in thinking Miranda didn't lock Humphrey's cage!

"It appeared to be locked, but he was able to open it from the inside. He did the same thing to me that he did to Miranda," she explains.

He did? And he got caught?

"Humphrey has a new cage now, with a lock that works," Mrs. Brisbane says. "Most important, class, I want to publicly apologize to Miranda for wrongly accusing her and for not believing what she said was true. She is an honest person, and I hope she will accept my apology."

As she's talking, I watch my neighbor. He's standing near the cage door, staring hard at Miranda's face.

Miranda has never looked happier.

It takes a minute for me to figure it out. My pal Humphrey must have let Mrs. Brisbane see him out of his cage to prove Miranda's innocence. That little hamster deserves to have a town named after him—maybe even a whole country! He's as important in his own way as Lewis and Clark, Balboa and Neil Armstrong!

You need to be brave to do the right thing, no matter how hard it is. *That's* a hero!

Later, I'm floating in my tank when I notice a commotion in the classroom. Mrs. Brisbane has lost her glasses, and everybody in class is running around searching for them, with no luck.

They look as high as the top of the tall cabinet. They look as low as under their desks. But by the end of school, the glasses are still missing, and Mrs. Brisbane goes home upset.

Aldo comes and does his usual great job of cleaning, but even he doesn't find the glasses.

They have completely disappeared!

Maybe I could find them, but it's too dark for me to try my Neil Armstrong act. I decide that I will try in the morning.

The sun is barely shining when my neighbor wakes me up. He's not just squeaking, he's squeaking like I've never heard before—as loud a noise as any bellowing bullfrog ever made.

I have no idea why he's so excited, until I see that he's staring hard at the floor *way under* Mrs. Brisbane's desk. What in the swamp does he find so interesting?

I stare at the same spot for a long time. At first, I don't see anything . . . and then suddenly, I see something glittering in the early morning light. I can't believe my great big eyes. Those are Mrs. Brisbane's glasses!

We couldn't see them before, but now the sunlight is hitting them just right.

"BOING-BOING-BOING-BOING!" I tell Humphrey. "Don't worry! I'll get them!"

"SQUEAK-SQUEAK-SQUEAK!" he answers.

Of course, he's frustrated because he can't open his new cage door.

"I'll get them!" I tell him again, as I start popping the top of my tank.

Humphrey is still frantically trying to open his cage door.

"Don't give up! Try again!" I tell him. I'm pretty sure he could open *any* door if he tries.

Humphrey pushes the door as hard as a small hamster can, but it still doesn't open.

"Twist it! Twist it like this!" I tell him, leaping in the air and wiggling my body so he'll see what I'm saying. Even with all of the twisting, I'm still leaping high enough to shift the top of my tank.

Humphrey simply stares at me.

I keep on twisting this way and that—and tell him, "BOING-BOING-BOING-SCREEEE!"

If he doesn't get the point now, I don't think he ever will!

Now there's a big enough space at the top of my tank. I'm ready to leap to the floor to get the glasses.

I'm as nervous as a baby bird on its first flight. I might not be as fast as Humphrey. What if I get caught outside my tank? What if I get a new top that doesn't pop?

But I have to try, and I am about to take the big leap when Humphrey finally gets the message! After twisting the door latch back and forth and jiggling it up and down, he does something really smart. He gets underneath the lock, pushes up and then twists it to the right.

The door flies open, and he tumbles out onto the table.

"Way to go!" I cheer him on.

Humphrey pauses to look up at the clock. Class will be starting before too long.

I hold my breath, hoping he'll go for it. "You can do it, Humphrey! You can do it!"

Of course, he does! He slides down the table leg and starts to run, but Aldo has polished the floor and he slips and slides. It would almost be funny if it weren't dangerous. I think my heart stops beating for a second, but he picks himself up and *skates* across the floor to the desk, gliding and pushing with one paw and then another.

There's not much space between the bottom of Mrs. Brisbane's desk and the floor. I see now why the big tads and Aldo couldn't see the glasses. But Humphrey manages to slide under the desk.

I hold my breath again, because it seems like a long time before he reappears, but he does, this time pushing the glasses out into the open! HOP-HOP-HOORAY for Humphrey!

Someone will surely see them now. I only hope that happens before they get stepped on!

"Hurry! The bell's about to ring," I warn him. He must understand, because this time he slides on his stomach straight across the floor and manages to swing his way up to the table and get back in his cage just as the teacher enters. He made it!

But Mrs. Brisbane doesn't even notice the glasses. My heart sinks. Not only that: She's walking toward them and is about to step right on them—that's bad!

We both start screaming at her.

"SQUEAK-SQUEAK-SQUEAK! SQUEAK-SQUEAK-SQUEAK!"

"BOING-BOING! BOING-BOING! BOING-BOING!"

That stops her in her tracks, but she doesn't know why we're making so much noise.

And then she looks down. The smile on her face is worth all the energy Humphrey and I have put into trying to tell her.

She *is* puzzled about how they got out in the open. But the big tads are coming in the room, and luckily, she doesn't think about that mystery any more.

Humphrey, my hero, has done it again!

I probably *could* have leaped to the floor and pushed the glasses out . . . but maybe not fast enough to not get caught. In a way, I'm glad I didn't have to reveal my new secret skill. There's plenty of time for *that*.

🐾 🐾 🐾 🐾

My neighbor sleeps for most of the day—and I don't blame him.

He's sleeping when Mrs. Goldman comes in during recess—and she's not alone. Charlie is with her.

"Mrs. Brisbane, would it be all right for Charlie to say hello to Og?" she asks.

"Of course," my teacher says. "I know he'd love it!"

They slowly approach my tank. Charlie's eyes are fixed on me. What is that paper he is holding tightly in his hand?

"There he is, Charlie. This is where Og lives," Mrs. Goldman tells him.

"Og," Charlie says. "Og-Og-Og-Og."

"BOING-BOING!" I answer. "Good to see you!"

Mrs. Goldman explains that Charlie has drawn a picture of me.

"Thank you!" I boing.

"Show him, Charlie," Mrs. Brisbane says.

I can tell that Charlie isn't sure what to do. The room is very quiet.

And then he holds the picture up to my tank. "Og!" he says.

It's such a wonderful picture. I've only seen my reflection in the water, but it's a good likeness.

"I love it!" I tell Charlie, and I mean it. "BOING-BOING!"

"Frog. Friend," he says.

"YES!" I reply, and I can't help bouncing up and down.

"Bye!" Charlie says, and he turns to leave.

"Wait!" I say. I wish he would stay, but I'm awfully glad he came to see me. Charlie may not be a big talker, but he sure is great at drawing.

Humphrey hops on his wheel and squeaks cheerfully. I'm hoppy that he saw that frogs can help humans, too.

After school, Mrs. Goldman returns alone. "I want to tell you about Charlie," she tells Mrs. Brisbane. "Ever since Og's visit, he keeps drawing new frog pictures. And he's such a good artist—I didn't even know that until he met Og."

"Og is a special guy," Mrs. Brisbane says.

Who, me? My heart is singing. I hope Charlie comes to

see me again soon! I'd be hoppy to hold still while he draws more pictures of me.

I'm still thinking about Charlie when the families begin arriving to see Humphreyville. I'm hoppy to see that Paul and his family come, too.

So much happens, the evening is a blur. So many parents, grandparents, brothers and sisters come up to talk to me, I'm as surprised as a bat seeing sunlight.

"So, you are Og," a lady with a long braid down her back says. "Gail told me you inspired her to take charge of the animal hospital project. It's just what she needed to gain more confidence."

That must be Gail's mom.

"She did a great job!" I say, and she laughs at my boings.

Of course, Humphrey gets a lot of attention, too. After all, he's visited most of the big tads' homes.

And I jump for joy when Mandy's mom, Mrs. Payne, tells Humphrey she's sorry she thought he made her family sick.

"I can see what a healthy hamster you are," she tells my neighbor. "And because of you, my husband got his new job working for the vet!"

Mandy has a big smile on her face. "And I got my own hamster, Winky."

Way to go, Humphrey!

But the highlight of the evening is when Mr. Morales

drops in. I'm sorry Brenda and Willy aren't with him, but I overhear him telling Mrs. Brisbane about my visit to his house.

"I will be forever grateful to Og," he says. "For the first time, my children learned to appreciate each other and work together. I don't know how a frog made that happen, but believe me, he did."

My heart may burst with happiness.

At the end of the evening, Mrs. Brisbane announces that the following day, the students will be taking their buildings from Humphreyville home.

Home? You mean Humphreyville won't be here forever? You could knock me over with a butterfly wing!

Later, when Aldo comes in to take the extra chairs out and straighten the room, he pushes the table with Humphreyville up close to the table where Humphrey and I live. In the light streaming through the windows, it looks great, especially for a place made of boxes.

As soon as Aldo leaves, Humphrey flings open his cage door and scurries to the edge of the table, squeaking at me the whole time.

He's already lowering himself down to Humphreyville when I take a few huge leaps and pop the top of my tank!

"Wait for me!" I tell him.

I've done quite a bit of exploring lately, and now's my chance to explore this special little town named for my pal.

The Humphreyville table is only a few inches below

ours, so it's a simple hop for me, and I land right on the main street.

It's not easy to catch up with Humphrey, who scurries along, darting inside each building and then hurrying back out.

"Nice town, Humphrey," I tell him.

"SQUEAK-SQUEAK-SQUEAK!" he says. I think he's surprised and happy that I can get out of my tank.

I hop past Gail's yellow house and the pizza place, the courthouse and the school.

I can hardly believe this little town is going to be taken apart. Luckily, Mrs. Brisbane already took a lot of pictures and put them on the bulletin board.

But in a way, no one will ever forget Humphreyville, the town named for a helpful classroom pet.

I pause in front of the pet hospital and then hop over to get a good look at the sign that says OG THE FROG NATURE PRESERVE. I guess you could say it's named for a helpful classroom pet, too.

I helped Charlie and Paul. I helped Mandy, Gail, Seth and the Morales family.

I went exploring to try to find out more about the human world, and what did I discover?

I learned that humans are all very different. And sometimes, when they keep trying and take chances, they can do amazing things.

I discovered that I'm braver than I thought.

And I found a way to have even more great adventures!

It looks like Humphrey and I have our work cut out for us, and I wouldn't have it any other way.

I feel so hoppy, I can't help singing.

I've been searching for adventure,
'Cause I like to roam,
I've been searching for adventure,
Away from my safe home.
I have scaled the walls of castles
And swam across a moat.
I have learned about new places,
where someday I might float.

But even though I roam,
Even though I roam,
Even though I roam so far away,
Even though I roam,
Even though I roam,
I am here to stay!

"SQUEAK!" my friend chimes in.

I keep on singing, and Humphrey joins in. He doesn't know the words, but it doesn't matter.

Even though I roam,
SQUEAK-SQUEAK-SQUEAK-SQUEAK-SQUEAK,

Even though I roam so far away,
SQUEAK-SQUEAK-SQUEAK-SQUEAK-SQUEAK,

Even though I roam,
I am here to stay!
SQUEAK-SQUEAK!

Sing-Along Suggestions
🐾 🐾 for Og's Songs 🐾 🐾

All of Og's songs can be sung to familiar melodies. Have fun singing!

Page 4
How I love a mucky home . . . . "Mary Had a Little Lamb"

Page 12, 24–25
Rock-a-bye, frog friends . . . . "Rock-a-bye Baby"

Page 47–48, 53–54
I'm a prince . . . . "Three Blind Mice"

Page 57
Happy hatchday to you . . . . . "Happy Birthday to You"

Page 65
I've been yearning for adventure . . . . "I've Been Working on the Railroad"

Page 83, 93
Gone exploring . . . . "Oh My Darling Clementine"

Keep reading for a sneak peek into
Og's next adventure!

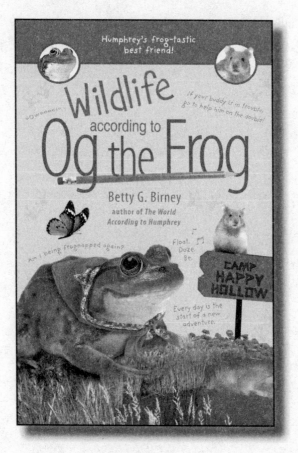

The End

· · · · · · · · · · · · · · · ·

*In the swamp, the only thing
that stays the same is change.*

—Granny Greenleaf's
Wildlife Wisdom

I can't believe it's happening to me again!

Just a few months ago, I was frognapped out of my home in the swamp—the only home I've ever known. I went from a life full of my lively green frog friends, classes with our teacher, the wise Granny Greenleaf, all the yummy insects a frog could dream of and long afternoons floating on a lily pad to my new life at Longfellow School.

The human world was strange at first, but I came to like the big tads in Mrs. Brisbane's class. I even became friends with a furry fellow whose cage is next to my tank. Humphrey is his name, and he's the other classroom pet in Room 26.

Now, just as I've learned the ins and outs of being a classroom frog and have come to love this new life, it's over! Gone!

And I have no idea what comes next.

It all begins on a warm day, when I am gazing out the window at the blue sky. Our teacher, Mrs. Brisbane, suddenly says, "Just four days until the end of school."

I am as shocked as a bat in bright light!

I'd think I didn't hear her correctly, except for the fact that Humphrey also squeaks in alarm.

"SQUEAK-SQUEAK-*SQUEAK*!" he cries out. He's a squeaky little hamster, but he has a big heart.

"I can't believe it!" I say, even though I know Humphrey and the big tads only hear the twangy sound I make: "BOING-BOING!" They think it's funny.

After the students leave for the day, Mrs. Brisbane comes over to our table by the window. She is humming happily.

"I guess you fellows are wondering what you'll be doing when school is over," she says with a grin.

Humphrey lets out another series of SQUEAK-SQUEAK-SQUEAKs, and Mrs. Brisbane explains that it's a surprise.

Surprises like a tasty mosquito who flies right into my mouth are nice. But I don't like surprises like hungry snapping turtles with huge jaws. Especially Chopper, who also lived in the swamp with me.

I don't think Humphrey likes surprises of *any* kind.

Once we're alone, my neighbor is quiet until it gets dark and Aldo comes in to clean Room 26, as he does on every weeknight.

He's extra cheery as he goes to work. He tells us that school is already over for him, and he got good grades.

Aldo is bigger and older than the big tads, but he still goes to school to learn to be a teacher like Mrs. Brisbane.

Tonight, he cleans the room as he's never cleaned it before. He whistles, twirls his broom and practically dances across the floor. When he settles down to eat his sandwich, he tells us, "When Longfellow School closes next week, I'm leaving town!"

Aldo seems pleased about leaving, but I see Humphrey's tail twitch and his whiskers droop.

When we're alone again, Humphrey crawls into his little sleeping hut, and I don't see him again the rest of the night. Poor guy. He loves school so much, and now so do I.

It's time to float in the water and let my thoughts wander.

I can almost hear Uncle Chinwag back in the swamp, saying, "Float. Doze. *Be.* And you will live so happily."

But I'm not feeling so hoppy tonight, so I dive into the water side of my tank and splash around until I am as tired as a hummingbird flying against a heavy wind.

Then I hop back up on my rock and go to sleep.

When our principal, Mr. Morales, visits our classroom, he seems as happy about the end of school as Aldo and Mrs. Brisbane are. He and his family are going to "hit the road," he says. I think it means they are leaving town, too.

Mrs. Brisbane explains that she and her husband are going to Tokyo, where their son is getting married. That's a long way from here. Are Humphrey and I going, too? Is that the surprise?

"SQUEAK-SQUEAK-SQUEAK!" By now, I know those are squeaks of alarm.

Our future is as mysterious as the Great Unknown, as we called the world beyond the swamp.

Over the next few days, the students in Room 26 are as busy and buzzy as bees in a field of flowers. There are reports to be graded, desks to be cleaned out and books to return to the library.

But why does school have to end? And where will that leave Humphrey and me?

Speaking of Humphrey, I don't know what in the swamp he's thinking, but I do know his busy brain is always working.

Once we're alone that night, the little fellow jiggles his lock and scampers over to my tank.

"SQUEAK-SQUEAK-SQUEAK! SQUEAK-SQUEAK-SQUEAK!"

Then he scrambles to the edge of the table and slides down the leg, as fast as an eagle swooping down on a lizard. That's *fast*.

Still moving quickly, he hurries across the floor, then flattens himself so he can slide under the door and out into the hallway.

"Be careful, Humphrey!" I try to warn him. But it's too late. He's gone.

I don't see Humphrey again for a long time.

I should be used to watching him go off on a nighttime adventure. He does it often.

Truthfully, I'm a little jealous. I'm an adventurous guy, too. I'd like to go exploring at night, the way he does. But I can't slide down the table leg, squeeze under the door or let myself dry out.

So, I'm left behind. And every single time, I'm as nervous as a mouse listening to the midnight hoots of an owl until he comes back.

While I wait, I dive into my water and swim laps, wondering what my furry friend could be doing all this time. Where can he be? What is he thinking?

A song drifts into my head, and as I often do, I calm myself by singing.

Humphrey loves to help his friends,
He's a daring class pet,

But he is roaming far away,
And he has not come back yet.

Humphrey Hamster, please come home,
Humphrey Hamster, hurry!
If you are not back here soon,
I will turn gray with worry!

My tank isn't big, so I swim a *lot* of laps before Humphrey finally crawls under the door again.

"BOING-BOING!" I welcome him. But he still has hard work ahead of him.

Since Humphrey can't slide *up* the table leg, he grabs onto the blinds' cord and swings back and forth, higher and higher, until he's level with the table. Then he lets go and leaps onto the tabletop. Now, *that's* something I'm good at: leaping.

"Welcome back!" I greet him again.

Humphrey doesn't answer. I can tell he's really tired by the way his tail is dragging.

However, he's not too tired to take out the tiny notebook hidden behind the mirror in his cage and scratch away with his little pencil.

Scritch-scritch-scritch!

Poor guy. I wish he could chill out.

I float in the water again, trying to relax, but I keep wondering: Where did my pal go tonight?

6

On the last day, it seems as if one minute Mrs. Brisbane is taking attendance, and the next thing I know, she's checking to see that the big tads have emptied their desks.

Late in the day, the door opens and someone unexpected enters. I know her, of course. I remember her bouncy dark curls and her smiling face.

The big tads cheer loudly when she arrives, but Humphrey is unusually silent. That surprises me, because the one thing I know about Ms. Mac is that she and Humphrey are special friends.

In fact, I think he loves her.

"Am I too early?" Ms. Mac asks.

Mrs. Brisbane says her timing is perfect.

Then Ms. Mac speaks to the big tads about their summer plans, which is nice.

But the next words she says change everything.

"I just want you to know that your friends Humphrey and Og are going to have a fantastic summer, too. Because they are coming with *me*!"

I don't know where Ms. Mac is taking us, but at least I know someone will be looking out for us, and I whoop out, "BOING-BOING-BOING-BOING-BOING!"

Ms. Mac laughs and then says something that makes my heart leap. "We are going to have a *great* adventure!" she announces.

Before I know it, the bell rings and the big tads rush out, with Garth in the lead, as always.

Humphrey squeaks a farewell, and he's still squeaking as I take a deep dive off my rock. It's cooling and calming in the water, so I can think about what just happened: the end of school.

Then I remember Granny Greenleaf saying, "If you think more about where you've been than about where you're going, you'll never get anywhere."

At least Humphrey and I are going *somewhere*, and we're going there with Ms. Mac.

I like her a lot. When she comes into the room, she's like a breath of fresh air. Besides the fact that Ms. Mac is nice, all I know about her is that long before I came to school, she was substituting for Mrs. Brisbane. She's the human who went to the pet shop and brought Humphrey back to Room 26.

She picked him out . . . and that's why they have a special friendship.

It was a good decision to make Humphrey a classroom pet.

But then a funny little thought hops into my head: Ms. Mac has known Humphrey a lot longer than she's known me. She knows *he'll* have a wonderful summer. But what about me?

The first thing I learn about Ms. Mac is that she doesn't waste time. She says good-bye to Mrs. Brisbane, and in a flash, we're on our way.

I'm not sure where we're going, but at the rate Ms. Mac is moving, we'll get there quickly. She's as peppy as a frog who swallowed some bees. Believe me, nothing can get you hopping like swallowing a couple of buzzing bees.

Ms. Mac lives in an apartment, which means there are different homes grouped together in one building. Her apartment is full of nice bright light and colorful pictures on the wall.

"Welcome back, Humphrey!" Ms. Mac places his cage on a big round table. "You remember living here before?"

Humphrey answers with a happy squeak.

So, he lived here before? I always thought Ms. Mac brought him directly from the pet shop to school. They know each other even better than I thought.

Once we're settled, Ms. Mac checks Humphrey's cage to make sure everything is in its right place. "There, Humphrey. Your mirror and hamster wheel are right where you like them," she says. "And you have nice clean water."

"SQUEAK-SQUEAK-*SQUEAK*!" he thanks her.

Ms. Mac inspects my tank next. "Hmm," she says. "I'm not sure exactly where things go, Og. And I have a little trouble understanding you. But I'll learn."

"BOING-*BOING*!" I answer.

She chuckles. "No wonder the children say you're funny!"

"I'm not trying to be funny," I respond. "I'm trying to talk!"

This time, she starts to laugh, then she stops herself and leans toward my tank. "I'm sorry, Og. I'm not laughing at you. I think you have a fabulous voice," she says.

"You should hear me sing," I tell her.

She smiles at my boings, but she doesn't laugh again. "I don't know much about frogs," she tells me. "But I have a book, so I can figure out exactly what you need."

She holds it up. It's a big thick book. I hope she's a fast reader, because I'm a little hungry.

Luckily, the food section is near the front of the book, and I get some tasty mealworms for dinner. Not as nice as a juicy cricket, but least I'm not hungry anymore.

❦ ❦ ❦

The days at Ms. Mac's are quiet, except for the music that is almost always playing in the background.

Some nights, Ms. Mac makes a maze on the floor and lets Humphrey out of his cage. He is good at running through mazes, especially if there are a few sunflower seeds at the end.

"I'd take you out, Og, but I'm not sure if you should be out of the water," she tells me.

I think she needs to read faster.

One day, she does a thorough tank clean, following the book step by step, and she cleans Humphrey's cage as well.

At least I'm in good hands, but I'm not sure I'll ever be as close to Ms. Mac as Humphrey is.

So far, it's a good summer, although I don't see it as the great adventure Ms. Mac mentioned the day she took us home.

A nice, cozy break, yes. A great adventure, no.

Then one evening, the music gets turned up and the doorbell starts ringing. Before I know it, Ms. Mac is introducing us to a parade of friends, many of them carrying dishes and bowls full of food.

"Dion, Annie, Marcus—meet Humphrey and Og!" She brings them over to our table.

"Oooh, what a fine-looking frog," the woman called Annie says. "And the hamster is adorable!" she adds.

We meet even more friends. Andre, Evelyn, Joe. They all linger around the table to "ooh" and "ahh" over Humphrey and me.

"SQUEAK!" my neighbor greets them.

"BOING-BOING!" I add.

The man called Andre says, "That was original!"

"Thank you," I boing.

I have spent many boisterous evenings in the swamp with the sounds of howling, chirping and hooting. But this evening at Ms. Mac's is every bit as noisy as that—without the annoying RUM-RUMMINGs of the bullying bullfrogs.

As the music goes on, the dancing begins. More people come through the door. Vic from next door and Maura from downstairs arrive and, well, I lose count of all the guests.

And then I hear it. BEAT-BEAT-BEAT. BONGA-BONGA-BONG!

Ms. Mac is bringing out some drums—a pair of them—and pounding out a beat.

"How do you like these bongo drums, Og?" she asks.

"Bongo?" I ask. My whole head vibrates at the sound of that word, because Bongo was my name back in the swamp! But Ms. Mac doesn't know that.

BONGA-BONGA-BONG! she plays.

I can't help but join in. "BING-BANG-BOING!" I twang.

The crowd loves it.

"Go, Og!" someone cries.

Ms. Mac plays a little louder and a little faster.

"BING-BANG-*BOING*!" I repeat.

The crowd cheers. I think I hear some piercing SQUEAKs in the background.

I start hopping to the beat of the drum. The sound reminds me so much of warm summer nights in the swamp, when all the creatures are at their noisiest.

The background music is the constant chirping of the crickets and the loud, deep voices of the bullfrogs going, "RUM-RUM-RUM-RUM!" Owl hoots and the high-pitched "kee-aahs" of hawks add to the night music, along with the beat of the woodpecker drumming away at a nearby tree. RAT-A-TAT-A-TAT!

Once, a chorus of green frogs even sang a song about me! My heart swelled with pride.

I don't usually sing in front of humans, but I can't help myself.

> There was a swamp where lived a frog
> And Bongo was his name-o.
> B-O-N-G-O!
> B-O-N-G-O!
> B-O-N-G-O!
> And Bongo was his name-o.

Everyone's dancing now, except Ms. Mac, who is pounding those drums.

I glance over at Humphrey's cage. He's hanging from the top bars of his cage, squeaking his lungs out. "SQUEAK-SQUEAK-SQUEAK-A! SQUEAK-SQUEAK-SQUEAK-A!"

"More, Og, more!" the humans shout.

So, I give them more.

> And in a classroom lived that frog
> And Bongo was his name-o.
> B-O-N-G-O!
> B-O-N-G-O!
> B-O-N-G-O!
> And Bongo was his name-o.

The sound was deafening, but the neighbors didn't care because they were all at the party, too!

The festivities keep going for a long time. And when the music stops, Humphrey is nowhere to be found.

"Humphrey, where are you?" Ms. Mac scurries around the apartment looking for him.

I hear a weak squeak, and when she checks his cage, she spots him in his sleeping hut.

"Sleep well," Ms. Mac whispers to him.

She comes over to my tank and flashes a big smile. Nobody smiles quite like Ms. Mac. "You were certainly the life of the party, Og," she says.

"You weren't so bad yourself," I reply.

"You'd better get some sleep, Mr. BING-BANG-BOING, like your friend Humphrey, because we've got a big trip coming up," she says.

"Where are we going?" I ask.

"For some folks, vacations mean relaxing and doing nothing," she explains. "But me? I like an adventurous vacation where I see new things and meet new people. And animals," she says. "I have a feeling you do, too."

"Animals? What animals will we be meeting?" I ask.

She turns off the light and leaves the room before I get an answer. And she expects me to sleep tonight?

I cool off in the water for a while. I'm not sure if I am asleep or awake because the whole evening has seemed like one big, noisy, wonderful dream.

Road Trip

. . . .

I watch every move Ms. Mac makes the next day. She washes and sews, sorts and folds clothes, always humming a happy tune. I wish she'd get those bongo drums out again.

She pulls a suitcase out of the closet and then . . . she leaves!

Humphrey and I don't say much. We sit and wait, but nothing happens.

This is our great adventure?

Humphrey dozes off, and I hum a new verse to the song from last night.

There was a frog who got so bored
And Bongo was his name-o.

Yawn, yawn, yawn, yawn, yawn!
Yawn—

The door swings open, and Ms. Mac hurries in, her arms loaded with shopping bags. "Sorry I was gone so long," she says. "I had a lot to get, including more food for you two."

"Squeak!" Humphrey says.

"We won't be near a town," she explains. "I bet you guys will be as happy to get out in nature as I will."

BING-BANG-BOING! We *are* going somewhere wild. "Out in nature," she just said.

"SQUEAK-SQUEAK-*SQUEAK*!" my excited neighbor exclaims.

"The call of the wild must be answered," she adds with a grin.

I dive into the water and start swimming laps.

I grew up in the wild, and I'm going back to the wild tomorrow. Will there be a swamp? Will there be *my* swamp? Will there be lots of yummy crickets, mosquitoes, beetles and dragonflies? Will there be—

Screech-screech-screech!

I glance over at Humphrey, who is spinning on his wheel like crazy. I wish someone could fix that screech.

Until now, I haven't thought about his summer. He may not like being out in the wild. He might not like mosquitoes or dragonflies, not to mention bats, snakes and bullying bullfrogs.

Ms. Mac leans down by my tank. "Og, you know every-thing about living in the wild," she tells me. "But Humphrey . . ."

She looks over at his cage. He's spinning his wheel so fast, he's just a blur.

"He doesn't know anything outside the human world," she says.

Ms. Mac is right. I was so excited about being back out-side, I'd forgotten that Humphrey has always lived inside.

"I hope you'll look out for him," she continues.

You bet I will! "BOING-BOING! BOING-BOING!" I assure her. "I promise!"

More books about adventures in Room 26 by Betty G. Birney